Wood Mistletoe
The Miracle Series

Landria Onkka

outskirts
press

Wooden Mistletoe
The Miracle Series
All Rights Reserved.
Copyright © 2017 Landria Onkka
v3.0

This is a work of fiction. The events and characters described herein are imaginary and are not intended to refer to specific places or living persons. The opinions expressed in this manuscript are solely the opinions of the author and do not represent the opinions or thoughts of the publisher. The author has represented and warranted full ownership and/or legal right to publish all the materials in this book.

This book may not be reproduced, transmitted, or stored in whole or in part by any means, including graphic, electronic, or mechanical without the express written consent of the publisher except in the case of brief quotations embodied in critical articles and reviews.

Outskirts Press, Inc.
http://www.outskirtspress.com

ISBN: 978-1-4787-5189-2

Cover Photo © 2017 thinkstockphotos.com. All rights reserved - used with permission.

Outskirts Press and the "OP" logo are trademarks belonging to Outskirts Press, Inc.

PRINTED IN THE UNITED STATES OF AMERICA

This book is dedicated to the souls of the world who believe in the magical, who never lose their faith, and who are not afraid to go with their heart. You are the ones who bring light unto this Earth and hope to those who sometimes lose their way. You are a demonstration of why we are here in the first place. To experience life with all its challenges and all its joy, no matter what. Thank you, my angels!

It's funny that just about the time we become wise, when we start to 'get it,' it's time to leave. Some might think that to be cruel, but I realized at one point that it was the journey that was so important. The journey is what we miss because we're so busy trying to get to the end, the goal. There isn't an end, and the goal just keeps moving. Yet we live in non-acceptance, always trying to reach that perfect place. We avoid pain and disappointment. I am here to tell you that it is better to experience love and the pain of loss than, as they say, to never know it at all. There is no way to protect yourself from 'life happening.'

It took a while for me. To find peace in the journey, that is. Some never make peace and die unfulfilled, always seeking. We receive and we experience loss. That is simply the nature of life. When, I wonder, did we stop accepting loss and view it as something bad? When did we decide that there was no value in it? To be human! It's a challenge. We miss so many of the small things, the important things, that make it so incredible. Like the flower outside the window that displays colors that man, on his own, could not conceive of. There is magic in the power of the universe. Magic beyond our comprehension. My advice is to always go with your heart, no matter what. For although the final result may not be what we had hoped for, it is ultimately always what we need. Never fear what will come, because everything is exactly as it should be. And it's wonderful.

Chapter One

"Where are you off to?" Sophie asked as she leaned over the nurse station, sticking her head past the counter.

"Going to get Miss Alexis and take her out to the garden," Annabel answered as she swished by on her way down the hall.

"Well, I'm glad to hear that," Sophie responded with a smile. "I was getting worried about her."

"Don't I know it. It's not like Miss Alexis to be so tired, it bein' Christmas time and all. I'm glad to see her gettin' her second wind!" Annabel said as she stopped and straightened her uniform top, smoothing out a wrinkle. "She does love Christmas!" Annabel, a tall attractive, middle-aged black woman exuded a southern ease about her. "Yep, she shor' does love Christmas!" She ran her hands over her hair which was neatly pulled off her face in a French twist.

"Miss Annabel, you're looking quite pretty with your fancy hairdo and pink lipstick!" Sophie commented as she watched Annabel ready herself before proceeding down the hall.

"Miss Alexis gave me the lipstick! An early Christmas gift. Said it's my stocking stuffer. It's called Pouty Pink." She pursed her lips and kissed the air. "She showed me how to do my hair too. It's a French twist!" Annabel turned toward Sophie, walked backward, stopped and dramatically pushed her hip out. She then proudly primped her hair.

"Ooo la la!" Sophie exclaimed, laughing.

Annabel joined in the laughter as she continued down the hall before stopping at a door. She gave a small knock then opened it. "Miss Alexis, it's Annabel, here to get you."

"Oh, good!" An attractive, elderly woman with perfect makeup and silver hair sat up in her bed. Propped up with European pillows, surrounded with expensive, Belgian Linen bedding, she began to push herself toward the edge of the bed. "Come in, dear! Come in!"

Annabel opened the door wide and stepped into the small room. "Miss Sophie noticed my French Twist," she said, sweeping her hand over her hair and turning her head to show off the back of her head.

"And, why wouldn't she? You look very pretty, Annabel. That French Twist suits you," the woman smiled as she readied herself.

"Now aren't you lookin' all pretty yourself!" Annabel complemented the elderly woman as she walked to her bedside. "Miss Alexis, are you sure you're feelin' well enough to visit the garden? It's a bit chilly out there and you've been real weak lately," Annabel asked. She walked to a wheelchair parked in the corner of the room and rolled it to the bedside.

"Oh, Annabel, don't you fret over me. I'm a very old woman, and something's got to kill me. I'd rather it be fresh air than pining away in my room!" she answered.

"I should know better than to argue with Miss Alexis!" Annabel grinned with a smile, as she locked the wheels of the chair and helped the frail woman into it. She then pulled a throw around the woman's shoulders and took a second one off the bed which she tucked around her legs. Annabel walked to a large wardrobe, opened the doors and pulled out a soft carry case which she attached to the back of the wheelchair. "We're all set," she announced.

"Well then let's be on our way," Miss Alexis ordered as she settled into the chair.

The women made their way past the nurse station, waving to Sophie and continued to the end of the hall where Annabel opened two glass French doors. Upon securing them, she wheeled Miss Alexis through and onto a large stone patio overlooking a beautiful garden. Woods stretched for as far as one could see that rolled up the face of the surrounding mountains. Annabel parked the wheelchair and secured it.

"Now I told you it was chilly out here!" Annabel reminded Miss Alexis.

"Oh, it's lovely. I welcome crisp, December air," she responded, closing her eyes and taking a deep breath. "Mountain air! I do love it," she said taking another deep inhale.

"Will that do Miss Alexis?" Annabel asked as she repositioned the throw around the old lady's shoulders.

"Oh, Annabel, this is perfect. Now, you know what comes next," Miss Alexis said as she gave a girlish smile.

"I sure do. You hold on now." Annabel reached into the carry case she attached earlier and pulled out a bottle of wine and a glass. She handed the glass to Miss Alexis. "Now hold on to that while I get your wine ready. Lucky for me, this is a screw top!" The ladies laughed as Annabel unscrewed the bottle and poured some into the empty glass. "Your Pinot Noir," she smiled.

"My favorite." Miss Alexis cupped the glass with both hands, swirled it and stuck her nose inside the rim to sniff the bouquet.

"You have your sunset, your garden, and your Pinot Noir!" Annabel slid the bottle back in the bag and placed her hand on the elderly woman's shoulder.

"Annabel, you need to pour yourself a glass and join me," she insisted and patted her friend's hand affectionately.

"Oh, Miss Alexis, you know I can't do that." Annabel shook her head and zipped the bag shut.

"And why not? When do you get off work?" Miss Alexis wrinkled her forehead, speaking in an adult-to-child manner.

"In an hour," Annabel stated, placing her hands on her hips. "You know I can't be drinkin' on the job!"

"An hour huh?" Miss Alexis took a sip of wine. She looked at her friend and raised an eyebrow. "Tell you what. In an hour, you come join me for our own private wine tasting," she declared. "Just one small taste to celebrate the holiday season. And I won't take 'no' for an answer!"

"Well, since you put it that way," Annabel replied, taking her hands off her hips.

"Good! I knew I could talk you into it!" Miss Alexis grinned and looked longingly at the garden before her. Tiers of neatly placed boulders dotted with ground cover and moss, separated dormant vegetable and herb gardens. Stone pathways lead to sitting areas with cement benches and bird baths where an abundance of color and sweet smells would reappear in the Spring.

"Oh Annabel, I wish that I had my hands in that rich soil instead of looking at it." Miss Alexis continued to stare, watching as a cardinal swooped down in front of her and pecked at ground seeds.

"It's too cold Miss Alexis to be playin' in that dirt. Only a few months and you'll be back out there watchin' your birds and blooms!" Annabel placed her hand on the elderly woman's shoulder and affectionately squeezed it. "You need to reserve your strength now. There's still some sun left for you to enjoy. Sunshine will be good for you," Annabel assured her. "You just stay bundled and enjoy your wine now. I hear that you have a visitor coming."

Miss Alexis looked up at Annabel and beamed. "Yes, I do! Do we have an extra wine glass ready?"

"We shor' do, Miss Alexis! I never know when you're gonna have a visitor!" Annabel smiled.

"I'm always hoping," she teased. Miss Alexis. scanned her lap and checked the side pocket of the wheelchair. "Annabel, you know what I forgot to bring out here? How silly of me! Can you please go get it for me?"

"Oh, you forgot your favorite memento? Of course! I'll be right back." Annabel responded.

"No rush, dear. Just when you get the chance," Miss Alexis said as she leaned back into her chair and sipped her wine. "I'm just a sentimental fool you know."

"Oh, you aren't no fool Miss Alexis. I have my little items that I treasure. You know since my Mama went to meet the good Lord, I keep some of her things close by. Why I even have those old work shoes she wore, sittin' right in the same place she'd put them when she came home from work every night! Silly, isn't it?"

"Annabel, there is nothing silly about that. Your Mama was a good lady and a hard working one at that. I can see why those shoes are special." Miss Alexis looked at Annabel with a kind expression and extended her hand out. "I miss her, too." She squeezed Annabel's hand and the women were silent for a moment when suddenly Christmas music began to play over speakers. "Holiday music! How nice! Sophie must have put that on for us. Please thank her for me," Miss Alexis requested.

'*Blue Christmas*' began to play and Annabel cringed in horror. "Oh no! We don't need that!" she declared. "No sad Christmas music allowed here! I'm goin' in there and we're gonna' change this." Annabel quickly turned toward the door, determined to handle the situation.

"Annabel, stop," Miss Alexis said smiling. "It's Okay. It's not a sad song to me. It's a song about love. Although, I remember when I didn't always think that way." She looked off into the distance. "Oh, how things change, Annabel" she shook her head, "and how quickly. Life is to be savored. Like this wine. It is ever changing."

*****

'*Blue Christmas*' played as Alexis, a pretty, blond woman in her early 30's sat at her laptop computer perched on her large dining room table. Dressed in flannel pajamas, she cried as she viewed a picture of a Jack Russell Terrier and a small, metal box of cremations placed next to it. She wiped her pink, puffy eyes. She didn't bother putting on makeup or brushing her hair most of the time. What for? No one would see her, and if by chance someone were to get a glance, she didn't care. She remembered when she had more energy, bothered to dress up, and looked forward to each day. But that was before her parents died and shortly afterward her beloved, old dog, Skuttlebutt joined them. She was alone now and the only thing that she looked forward to was decorating the numerous Christmas trees that she displayed each year and shared with a handful of friends. It was easy to hide behind her computer and her stories.

"Thank God for good friends," Alexis said out loud, grabbing a tissue from a box in front of her as she blew her nose. She began to collect the crumpled tissues strewn across the table, as tears continued to roll down her rosy cheeks. Suddenly, a shadow darted past her.

"Skuttlebutt?" Alexis leaned across the table and looked around the room, examining the old, wood plank floor. "Skuttle?" She walked into the kitchen and searched, but saw nothing. The sun streamed through the paned window over the large, white farm sink, spotlighting the original 1930's black and white floor tiles. There was total silence in the room. Between sniffles, Alexis looked around her newly renovated kitchen, pleased with the months of painstaking work she had dedicated to it. Every piece from the large, marble top island, reclaimed wood salvaged from a local barn, vintage cupboards with hand forged pulls and tiles were carefully chosen by her. It was another project, a deviation, that kept her mind off life outside of her novels.

"Huh." She placed her hands on her hips and sighed. "I'm losing it," she whispered, shaking her head to clear it when she caught a movement out of the corner of her eye. Alexis turned to see a kitty staring at her through the glass door leading to her backyard deck. "Orange Kitty!" The cat continued to sit and stare as Alexis walked to the door and opened it. "Orange Kitty, you came back! Where have you been, you naughty boy? Get in here," she affectionately scolded the small animal as she opened the door wider. The orange fuzzy cat casually sauntered into the kitchen, stretched, and arched before rubbing against her leg, purring.

Alexis opened a pantry door and searched the shelves, pulling out a can of cat food. She quickly scooped the smelly contents onto a small plate on the floor. The kitty carefully watched her and chatted loudly, sounding like a baby crow as he continued to weave back and forth against Alexis's legs, before tackling the gourmet meal.

"Orange Kitty, we're almost out of your favorite food," Alexis said as she viewed the cupboard where one lone can remained. The small cat purred as he continued to smack voraciously at the tasty treasure before him. "I'll be back!" Alexis, still in her pajamas, headed to a hall closet where she pulled out her long wool coat and winter boots. Grabbing her purse and keys, she headed to her vintage sports car parked in the driveway of her brick bungalow. She turned to examine the front garden where 'knock out' roses and other extensive flower beds sat dormant and bud-less.

The pristine, brick and stone fairytale home was her retreat and where she felt secure. It was one of the few things in her life that stood firm. Alexis had discovered the home while exploring the quaint, southern neighborhood. A bit neglected, she saw the possibilities and purchased it, renovating each room, restoring and preserving its charm. Yes, she was proud of her work and just looking at it made her feel grounded. It was her safe-haven, along with her stories. They were a passage to another world that she controlled, including the always happy endings.

It was unusually quiet. Most of the neighbors were at work, and the noise of mowers and lawn equipment that dominated the daytime hours of the warmer months was absent. The paved street lined with more bungalows revealed large porches, some with two person swings, others screened in with furniture, where neighbors gathered with a glass of wine or sweet tea. All were silent and waiting to be dusted off when Spring arrived.

Alexis planted herself in the bucket seat of her sports car and made her way, just like she always did twice a week, to the small grocery store nearby. The list was usually the same; cream, coffee, cat food, bottled water, and vegetables. She was relieved to see only a few cars in the parking lot and quickly grabbed a nearby shopping cart as she made her way inside. She could relax now. Surely none of her neighbors would be shopping this time of day. Besides, mostly elderly customers frequented the small store while the masses opted for the fancier food chain further down the street. Yes, this was another safe spot for Alexis. She relaxed and leaned on the cart as she slowly walked down each aisle, throwing in a box of crackers, hummus, and a block of cheese. Still hunched over her cart and shuffling, she arrived at the pet food aisle where an elderly woman stood, staring at the cat food shelves. Dressed in men's cargo pants, worn men's hiking boots and an oversized sweater, Alexis guessed that she might be a street person. Her grey thin hair was long and her tan face was weathered and cracked from her cheeks to her jawline resembling a dried creek bed.

"I'm not sure what to get," the old lady said out loud, startling Alexis.

Alexis was not sure if the comment was made for her or if she was simply talking to herself. It would be rude to ignore her. "You're not sure which cat food to buy?" Alexis asked keeping a safe distance. "How old is your cat?"

"I actually don't have a cat. I have a dog. I mean I had a dog! Oh, that sounds confusing. You see, I'm 90 and I was so worried about my dog. He was 18 years old and I was afraid that I would die before him." She gave Alexis a sad smile. "I'm so thankful that the good Lord took him first. I don't know where he would have gone if I had departed first. I'm alone, you see." The woman looked directly at Alexis, her kind eyes a washed-out blue.

"Oh, I'm so sorry. I know how devastating that can be," Alexis said, now feeling ashamed at her initial thoughts that the woman was perhaps homeless. She moved closer. "I just lost my Jack Russell. He was 16. It's tough."

"It is, and at my age, I can't even consider getting another dog. So, I just feed the stray cats," she shared. "*That* is why I'm buying cat food, you see. I don't know much about cats. Do you know about cats?"

Alexis paused. Chills ran up her arms. There, in some other reality, stood the future Alexis. She was suddenly aware that she was in public with her pajamas on. She quickly pulled her coat tighter to hide the pajama pants that were poking out of the bottom. But the older woman never looked down at them and instead, kept a concentrated gaze on Alexis's face. "I don't really know much about cats, myself. It's funny, but I'm feeding strays, also," Alexis laughed. "I can't bring myself to get another dog, either. It's a big commitment." Alexis stepped forward and examined the shelves, stocked with bags of indoor, outdoor, and numerous flavor choices. "Here," Alexis pointed to a bag.

"Oh! I was feeding them this one," the woman said pointing.

"That's for indoor cats. This is the one that I buy," Alexis shared. "It's the 13-pound bag and lasts longer. It's a good deal."

"Oh, then that's the one I'll buy." The elderly woman began to pull the bag off the shelf when Alexis quickly grabbed it and placed it in her cart.

"Thank you, dear!" The woman looked at her with a kind expression.

"My pleasure. You have a nice evening," Alexis said as she smiled. For a moment, they shared an unspoken connection.

"Geez," Alexis whispered once she gained some distance. "What am I doing?" It was suddenly glaringly obvious that she hadn't bothered to brush her hair or put on makeup. She wished that she had worn a hat or scarf to hide her puffy, naked face. She quickly grabbed several cans of cat food before pushing her cart to the checkout.

An attractive man standing in front of her gave her a curious glance. He quickly looked away and began to speak to the checkout clerk. "Are you ready for the holidays?" he asked.

"Sure am! Having the whole family over! Kids, grand kids, it's going to be a full house!" the cashier answered.

Alexis quickly placed her items on the conveyer, anxious to get out of the store. The gentleman grabbed his bags and headed out, giving Alexis another glance much like the look that she had initially given the old woman in the pet aisle. She quickly swiped her credit card.

"Back for your kitty food! Will you need help getting it into the car?" the cashier asked.

"No. No thanks, Gertie," Alexis said, as she grabbed the receipt and rushed to the parking lot hoping that she would not encounter another human. She jumped into her car and made her way home.

"I'm home!" Alexis shouted as she entered the front door with her grocery bags. There, near the entrance sat Orange Kitty. "I got your favorite food!" The cat meowed and followed Alexis into the kitchen, dodging in front and almost tripping her. The cat plopped down in the middle of the room and watched as she stashed the large bag of cat food in the pantry and unpacked her groceries.

Looking at the small stash of food, Alexis decided that she couldn't be bothered to prepare a plate. She proceeded to rip open a box of crackers and stuffed one in her mouth when she heard a knock on the front door.

"You decent?" shouted a woman.

"In the kitchen!" Alexis answered. A pretty red head with large, green eyes and long, thick lashes appeared in the kitchen doorway.

"Hi neighbor," Jill said as she walked to the counter and picked up a bag of Wasabi peas, examining them. "Dinner?"

"Don't be silly," Alexis laughed. "That's dessert. *This* is dinner," she smiled as she raised a block of cheese and the open box of crackers.

"Of course," Jill smiled. "Are you in your pajamas?"

"Maybe," Alexis said, trying to look busy.

"I'll bet you went grocery shopping and you still don't have anything to eat, do you." Jill walked to the refrigerator and opened it. "Oh, this is healthy," she said as she pulled out a bottle of champagne. She viewed the empty interior.

"I was celebrating," Alexis said as she leaned over, placing two tomatoes in a vegetable drawer.

"Celebrating what?" Jill asked as she placed the champagne on the counter.

"My next best seller," Alexis answered.

"That's nice Alex, but you can't live like this. Here," Jill said, handing her a small paper bag. "I made you some vegetarian chili."

Alexis opened the bag and removed a container. "You're so sweet," she said as she leaned over and hugged Jill.

"Not really. I have my own reasons for keeping you alive," Jill grinned. "Okay, girlfriend. I know you just came back from the grocery store and I'm serious. Be honest. Did you go out in your PJ's?"

"I'm a writer, I don't need to get dressed. Besides, I wore my long, winter coat," Alexis said as she took another bite of a cracker, giving Jill a grin.

"I know. That's the problem. You're either in your workout gear or your PJ's." Jill paused, examining Alexis's face and hair. "I think that you're depressed," she said, pushing a tendril of hair off Alexis's face.

Alexis smoothed her hair back, then pulled down on her pajama top to straighten it out as she pushed her shoulders back and raised her head in a dignified stance. "I'm not depressed." She grabbed the box of crackers along with the block of cheese, a plate, knife, and walked into the dining room. "You coming?"

"Then what are these?" Jill said as she made her way to the tissue strewn dining table. Alexis shrugged her shoulders. Jill gently reached across the table and placed her hand on Alexis's as she attempted to slice open the package of cheese. "Listen, I know it's been tough losing Skuttlebutt, *but* — no pun intended — you need to get out once in a while and focus on other things," Jill said with a soft voice. Alexis sniffled. "Hey, I miss the Butt too." Jill said, patting Alexis's hand.

"Could you please not refer to him as the Butt." Alexis grabbed a tissue and wiped her nose, still sniffling. "Here," she said as she pushed the plate of cheese and crackers across the table.

"That's good. You sniffle and I'll prepare the cheese." Jill carefully finished opening the package and sliced the cheese into thin pieces. "You know, I miss Skuttles . . . er, Skuttlebutt, too. Now it's time to get out and face the world. I know it's all cozy in your little brick, 100-year-old home," Jill continued as she sat down at the table and placed a piece of cheese on a cracker.

"85"

"What?"

"It's only 85 years old," Alexis corrected her.

"Oh. OK, your 85-year-old cozy brick home. Venture out! Have some fun!" Jill patted her hand again.

Alexis spotted a shadow shooting by her feet. "Did you see that?" Alexis asked, as she pointed to the floor.

"See what?" Jill looked at the spot that Alexis pointed at.

"That, that thing that just went by. That like, a shadow or something. I keep seeing a shadow out of the corner of my eye!" Alexis continued to point.

"Okay, that's it. We're out of here." Jill stood and grabbed Alexis's arm.

"No really, I keep seeing this little thing that darts around the house," Alexis explained with a serious expression.

Jill looked at her as if she was insane. "Come on! Out! We're going out! Get dressed. We're getting you out of this house."

"Okay, Okay! Just wait a minute. It's time to take Willow for a walk. Want to come with?" Alexis walked to her coat, laying on the sofa.

"In your pajamas and robe?" Jill asked.

"No, silly, this isn't my robe, it's my overcoat. And I'll put on my boots. Come on, no one will know!" Alexis pulled on her coat and twirled. "See? You can't even tell."

Jill sighed. "If it'll get you out of here, I'll go along with this." Jill pulled on her own coat following Alexis out the door as she shook her head in disbelief. They headed across the driveway to the neighbor's house where Alexis unlocked the front door. Inside, a white, lab puppy happily jumped on them, licking their hands and wagging her tail at the sight of the visitors.

"This is all I need," Alexis said hugging the dog.

"Oh boy," Jill sighed, petting Willow and frowning.

Willow happily allowed Alexis to attach her leash and the three made their way down the driveway and to the street. The chubby puppy attempted a sprint when possible then stopped to sniff every bush and plant within reach. The women walked in silence, watching the pup pounce and explore.

"It's nice that you take your neighbor's pup for walks," Jill commented, "but Alexis."

"I love it just as much as Willow does. I'm just not ready to get another dog, you know?" Alexis responded.

"Yeah, I totally understand," Jill said and paused for a few minutes before continuing. "How is your Grandmother?"

"Oh, some days she's coherent and other days she doesn't know who I am. Funny, but it's like she lives in another dimension. The good part is that wherever she exists, it's a peaceful place."

"Is she still talking to people on the other side?" Jill asked.

"She talks to my Dad. Oh, and Michael visits her." Alexis gave Jill a big grin.

"Who's Michael?" Jill's interest perked up.

"You know, Archangel Michael." Alexis raised an eyebrow.

"Oh really? *The* Archangel Michael? I wish I was a fly on the wall for those conversations." Jill smiled. "It seems like a peaceful existence. I mean if you're going to be delusional, at least she has visitors."

"Yeah, that's true. I don't know what to make of it. Sometimes she shares senseless jabber and other times, incredibly wise information that she says comes from Michael. It's as though she exists in dual worlds." Alexis gave Willow's leash a gentle tug, guiding her off a neighbor's lawn.

"So have you asked any questions?" Jill asked with a serious expression.

"You mean Michael? Are you joking?" Alexis paused as she examined Jill's face for a hint of a smile, but found nothing. "You mean to humor her?" Alexis frowned.

"No! It's possible that you could have direct access to a very important person, uh, I mean Angel!" Jill responded. "If your Gran has a direct connection to Michael, you need to take advantage of that!" Jill nudged her.

"Dear Lord, you *are* serious! Jill, that is ridiculous," Alexis snickered.

"Who says? Just because you don't see him, doesn't mean he isn't there, having a good ol' chat with Mary." Jill nodded with confidence.

"Let me just clarify what I'm hearing. Are you saying that you believe that my Gran is speaking to Archangel Michael in her room at the Assisted Living home?" Alexis turned to look her directly in the eyes with an expression of disbelief.

"Why not? I mean you're the one with the great imagination." Jill watched Alexis as they continued to walk, waiting for a response. Willow explored more bushes and lawns.

"I have to admit that I like the idea, but Jill, my Gran has dementia. Every other time I visit, she doesn't know who I am. She doesn't have a clear mind," Alexis reminded her.

"I know, but anything's possible, right? Or don't you believe your own fantasies? Is that all just stuff on paper?" She raised one eyebrow.

Jill had been a rock for Alexis for many years. She was the kind of friend that anyone would wish for, who accepted her without judgment, offered support and kind words, but provided a reality check when needed. She stood by Alexis through the best times of her life and recently the worst. It was Jill who showed up with soup and a bottle of wine when Alexis lost her parents. It was Jill who sat with her and cried when Skuttlebutt passed. She offered valued friendship beyond any price, to be respected and taken seriously.

"I never thought of it that way, but maybe I *don't* believe my own 'stuff.' I did once." Alexis hooked her arm in Jill's. "You're right. What you're saying does make sense. It really does." She stopped, allowing Willow to explore and paused to think deeper. "I'm going to try to open up my mind. Who's to say that Gran doesn't have a connection that I don't understand, right?"

"Do you mean that? I mean, you're not just humoring me?" Jill asked.

"No! I'm not, I promise. Maybe she *does* speak to Michael and my Dad and who knows who else." Alexis placed a hand on Jill's shoulder. "I'll tell you what. Next time I see her, and Michael makes his presence known, I'll ask a question or two. He already seems to have definite opinions about me! That's for sure," Alexis grinned.

"Are you serious? What did he say?" Jill was riveted, in anticipation of the answer.

"His favorite line is to *go with my heart*," Alexis shrugged her shoulders.

Jill frowned. "I don't follow you."

"Well, when I'm asking my Gran advice on one of my stories he butts in on our conversations frequently. Seems to think that if I go with my heart, I'll get the answers I need."

"Really? See? Now that *has* to be Michael! Who else would say something so simple and direct? Next time you see him, or I mean your Gran, ask if Jill should date Andrew. Oh wait, he's probably going to tell me to go with my heart. In that case, I'll take a pass." Jill paused. "Yeah, scratch that. I have more important questions to ask. Let me put some thought into it."

"Yeah. If you have to ask, you already have your answer," Alexis grinned. "In fact, I can answer that one for you!" They both laughed. "Let me know if you come up with a more serious question and I'll give it a shot."

"How interesting. I envy her," Jill paused. "Think about it. She's sitting in that Assisted Living home, by herself with only her granddaughter to visit her, yet she has this whole other exciting world! She has friends, she talks to people that have passed. She has divine access!"

"I agree. She's oblivious and at peace," Alexis continued. "You know the funny thing is that I think I get more out of our visits than she does. Thank goodness she doesn't know what I'm saying half the time." Alexis suddenly looked sad.

"Why is that?" Jill leaned down and pet Willow who jumped up and down as though on a trampoline.

"Well, I read my novels to her and work out plot issues. It's meaningless in the big scheme of things. I'm sure she doesn't have a clue what I'm talking about, but she's a great listener. Sometimes we need that, you know?"

"You always have me!" Jill placed her arm around Alexis's shoulder and squeezed it.

"I wouldn't do that to you, my friend. There aren't enough hours in the day to listen to my stories." Willow stopped and squatted to pee.

"You know, you're fortunate, Alexis. Your Gran is under good care with people at her side 24/7. I spent many years, as you know, looking after my Mother before she died. It takes a real toll on one's spirit. She wasn't quite the happy lady your Gran is," Jill shared.

"I know. I don't know how you did it." Alexis said.

"Well, you love them, so you cope. But, you get so entrenched in taking care of their needs that you can lose yourself along the way. Make sure that *you* don't lose yourself Alex. It's easy to hide from the world right now, so it's important to push yourself. Otherwise, we become complacent and fearful and believe me, it doesn't get better." Jill gave Alexis a serious look. "I know it's been tough losing your parents and Skuttlebutt all so close together, but it's important that you don't give up." Jill paused and continued. "When was the last time you went out on a date?"

"Ha! A date? Never. You know that. I have no interest, Jill. I have enough on my plate." Alexis tried to act uninterested in the conversation, leaned down and pet Willow.

"That's what I thought. What happened to that online dating service?"

"Oh, I checked it out and shut it down. It was stupid! And I don't have time." Alexis looked away to avoid eye contact.

"You have plenty of time. Hey, you don't have to get married. Just get out and have some fun! It'll force you to get dolled up and, trust me, you know it'll feel good."

"I know. I just can't get excited about it." Alexis forced a smile. She thought about her last relationship and how it ended with a slow fizzle. A nice guy who just wasn't a good match from the start, Alexis called it quits early. Relationships took commitment and, after all, her focus was her career. It was easier to be on her own with no complications.

Jill paused. "Hey, how's the mountain house coming along?"

"Oh, it's great!" Alexis was relieved to change the subject. "The structure is complete and I'm working on the details of the interior. I'll take you up there. We can visit the local wineries," Alexis said as she suddenly perked up.

"That sounds like fun. Just name the date," Jill said. "You know

Christmas is just around the corner. We can build a fire and decorate the place."

"Yeah, that'd be great. Why don't you come with me and visit some of those boutique Blue Ridge stores? I'd love to get some vintage and handmade pieces for the study and living area. Maybe buy some Adirondacks for the patio and get a cool piece of wood for the mantel."

"Twist my arm! I love to shop!" Jill was now getting excited.

"Then you're with the right girl. I have a whole list to tackle," Alexis shared.

Jill grinned as she looked Alexis up and down. "Not in the PJ's, I hope." Alexis recoiled at the comment. "Don't be too hard on yourself. We all go through stuff and you've taken on a lot. You're in a funk, that's all," Jill assured her.

"Oh, is that what this is?" They walked in silence for a few minutes. Willow stopped, stretched and yawned, then resumed her sniffing expedition. "Hey, let's get back. It's getting dark," Alexis said. The friends made their way to Willow's home, placing her safely inside.

"So, my guess is that you don't have any plans for dinner?" Jill asked as she stepped inside Alexis's living room.

"A dear friend of mine just happened to drop off vegetarian chili! Want to stay?" Alexis took off her coat and sat back in front of her computer.

"That chili is for you. Get back to your writing and I'll check in with you this week. What does your schedule look like?" Jill asked knowing full well what the answer would be.

"Working out, grocery shopping and back here. Oh, and I'll be visiting my Gran too," Alexis shared.

"Well, send her my love. I need to visit her soon. I want to hear what Angel Michael has to say. Maybe he can give me some investment tips," Jill smiled.

"Right," Alexis logged into her computer. "I'm sure that's a top priority for him. Hey, thanks for the chili." She paused and gave Jill a smile. "And thank you, my friend, for caring."

"You're very welcome. I'll pop in later in the week." Jill walked to the door and turned back around. "And get out of those PJ's!" She quickly exited, closing the door behind her.

Chapter Two

"So, Gran should Melanie and Victor break up or should he go missing under mysterious circumstances?" Alexis thought for a moment, and stared at the ceiling before continuing. Her Grandmother remained silent. "I think that Victor may have to have an accident. Maybe suffer from amnesia or something," she paused. "Yeah, that will be much easier. It'd be tough to explain how he disappeared then figure out how to write him back into the story down the road. This is much better don't you think, Gran?"

A frail, elderly woman sat tucked in her bed facing a television in a shelving unit on the opposite wall. Lights flashed as the scenes on the screen changed. Although the sound was turned off, she watched it intently. The small room was elegantly appointed with a love seat and two chairs, dresser, and side tables that held small lamps. A large window invited in the bright Georgia sun which filled the space. Alexis sat in a comfortable chair next to the bed. A small table situated in front of her held her laptop computer, open and ready. The letters on the keyboard were worn, although the computer was fairly new. Alexis sprayed a small cloth with a solution and carefully swept it across the screen, wiping away smudges.

"Michael says that you should go with your heart," her Grandmother responded.

"My heart, my heart. Oh, right. That seems to be Michael's standard answer lately." Alexis placed her finger to her cheek and thought for a moment. "Yeah, then I think amnesia is the way to go." Alexis pulled her chair closer and began to type on her computer then stopped. She looked at her Grandmother, cocked her head to one side and squinted her eyes. "Gran, who's Michael again?"

"The Angel, silly. He's right there," she pointed to the corner of the room.

"Oh right, Michael as in Archangel. Sorry, I was just checking. I forgot for a moment," Alexis smiled at her Grandmother, amazed at the consistency of her delusion.

"What other is there?" Her Grandmother nodded at the corner with a look of delight.

"Okay, so back to Melanie. Does she stick with Victor at his bedside or does she falter, you know, get tempted, maybe falls for the attending physician." Alexis stared out the window in thought, tapping her computer surface.

"You know your Father is much funnier on the other side." Her Grandmother giggled.

"Mary Bradford, are you saying that my Dad, your son, is funny?" Alexis stopped and stared at her Grandmother with a grin.

"Yes, does that surprise you? We continue to learn on the other side, you know." Grandma nodded her head with a 'matter of fact' expression.

"Well, I wish that I could hear all of this, Gran. I seem to be missing out on some real fun," Alexis teased.

"You are, my dear. You are!" Gran laughed. "You can join in any time, Alexis."

"Except that I don't seem to be much fun lately." Alexis became silent for a moment and once again stared out the window that overlooked a field of tall weeds and grass. "Okay, so back to Melanie."

"Michael said he already told you. Go with your heart. Always go with your heart," Grandma reminded her.

Alexis looked at the blank corner of the room where her Grandmother's gaze was now fixed. She examined the space thoroughly looking for even the slightest shadow or movement. There was none.

"Oh, I can't tell her *that*!" Grandma continued her conversation with the invisible entity.

"Tell me what?" Alexis asked her Grandmother, still examining the blank corner. "What? Tell me what?"

"I don't think you should hear this," Grandma responded, looking serious.

"No, I should. I really should! Right Michael?" Alexis said as she gestured to the invisible guest.

"Oh, all right, but that Michael can be very direct! You may not like this," Grandma announced.

"That's Okay, Gran. I can take it." Alexis sat straight in her chair with a sarcastic expression, folded her arms, and waited.

"Well, Michael says that you should start living those stories instead of writing them." Her Grandmother looked at Alexis with an 'I told you so' expression.

"*Michael* said that?" Alexis's mouth dropped open. "Michael the *Angel*? Are you sure that's Archangel Michael and not some other Michael?"

"Oh, I'm sure, Alexis. I told you he can be direct." She shook her head.

"No kidding." Alexis pouted. "Ouch! That was harsh! Anything else I need to know? I mean while he's giving out advice?" Alexis squinted her eyes and pursed her lips.

"Yes, but I don't understand this one." Grandma paused then spoke to the corner of the room. "Oh, alright, but I have no idea what you're talking about." She turned toward Alexis. "I think he's having a bit of fun with us," she said, looking apologetic.

"Oh now Michael's making jokes? Bring it on, Grandma. It couldn't be worse than the last comment." Alexis leaned forward, placed her elbows on the table before her and rested her head on her hands.

"He said that you should pay attention to the mistletoe. It will be your sign." She paused and listened to the silent speaker. "He also says that you shouldn't make *fun* of the mistletoe."

"Who would make fun of mistletoe?" Alexis looked puzzled. "Seriously?" Alexis realized that the conversation had taken an even more bizarre turn and that she was somehow a willing participant.

"I don't know. He said that you shouldn't make fun of the mistletoe. It will be your sign," Grandma smiled proudly as she repeated the message as though she had shared a clever riddle.

"My sign for what?" Alexis asked, now intrigued.

"Your fork in the road. But, you always have choice," she responded.

Alexis suddenly realized that she was having a conversation with someone who suffered from dementia and her unseen Angel friend. "Yeah, I know about that fork in the road. And I'll be sure that I don't make fun of the mistletoe." She looked around the room. "We're good to go here. No mistletoe in this room! And you can count on none being placed in my house! But if I should happen to run into any this holiday season, I'll be sure that I don't make fun of it!" She then turned to speak to the blank corner of the room. "Thanks there, Michael. I'll pay attention to that." Alexis let out a small giggle and went back to typing on her computer.

Her Grandmother spoke once again. "Yes she *did* listen." She paused as though listening and became noticeably agitated. "Now I think I know my Granddaughter very well, and I know that she will take your advice *very* seriously!"

"What? Now you're sticking up for me?" Alexis opened her mouth to pretend as though she was shocked.

"Well," Grandma shook her head and raised her eyebrows.

"Thanks, Gran. I appreciate it," Alexis stood and walked to her Grandmother, gave her a gentle hug, kissed her cheek, and returned to her writing. "Suddenly, I'm feeling inspired. It must be all of this Angel energy." She looked at her Grandmother who was now transfixed at the scenery outside of the window. A smile was on her face. "Gran, is there anything that I can get you?"

"Barbara, you don't have to do a thing. That little dog that was just in here is so cute! I hope that we get to see him again," Gran answered.

Alexis watched her for a moment and smiled. "That would be nice, Gran. I'm right here. If you need anything, you just let me know," she answered with a gentle tone.

A knock on the door interrupted the conversation. "Come in," Alexis turned to view the visitor. "Oh Mabel, hello. Come in! Come in! It's good to see you," Alexis greeted the Assisted Living attendant. A slender, black woman in her 40's, Mabel's face was kind and glowed with a peace that brought calm to anyone in her presence. She was one of the reasons that Alexis found the courage to place her Grandmother in the care of Creekside, along with the kindness of the entire staff. Mabel was practically family now and knew her Gran as well, if not better than she did at this stage in her life.

"I just came in to check on Miss Mary." She walked to the center of the room and looked at the elderly woman as she folded her arms. "How are you doing Miss Mary? Are you ready for your dinner yet?" Mabel asked in a southern drawl. Gran stared at Mabel with a confused and blank expression. "Miss Alexis, do you want to eat here in the room or shall we take Miss Mary down to the dining room?"

"Mabel, I think I'll take Grandma down to the dining room myself. If you can help me to get her into her wheelchair, I'd really appreciate it." Alexis requested as she closed her laptop.

"I sure can," Mabel said as she pulled out a wheelchair that was folded and stashed near the entrance.

"Mabel, you always look so happy. You glow like you're in love!" Alexis teased as she prepared her Grandmother.

"I am in love, Miss Alexis. I'm in love with the good Lord!" Mabel beamed.

"Well, you're in good company. We have Archangel Michael here who, by the way, has been doling out some advice today," Alexis winked at Mabel.

"Don't I know, Miss Alexis. That Michael, he visits Miss Mary *all* the time. She has an awful strong connection to get so many visits from Michael!"

Alexis shot Mabel a questioning glance.

"You think I'm crazy?" Mabel laughed. "I think Miss Mary has connections!" She stepped back and, once again, crossed her arms. "Miss Alexis, you don't believe? Shame on you!"

"Oh, my Gran has connections alright." Alexis shook her head, scooting her Grandmother to the end of the bed. Mabel and Alexis carefully shifted her to the wheelchair. Alexis reached for a shawl that rested on a nearby chair and wrapped it around her Gran's shoulders while Mabel gently placed slippers on her feet and positioned them in the steel foot holders.

"Now look at that," Alexis said as she stood back and examined her Grandmother with pride. "You look all pretty and ready for dinner. Are you comfortable?"

"Yes, but I need my lipstick, Dear," she answered, pointing to her purse on a nearby chair. "You never know who we'll meet!"

"Of course," Alexis responded, as she winked at Mabel, walked to the purse and rifled through the contents. "Here you go!" She raised a small, red silk bag, unzipped it and handed her Grandmother a tube of lipstick and compact.

Her Grandmother carefully opened the compact, and examined her face in the small mirror. She removed the lipstick cap and handed it to Alexis before puckering her lips and carefully coating them with color. She puckered again, tilted her head and nodded in approval.

"You look lovely, Gran," Alexis smiled as she took the items from her Grandmother and placed them back in the makeup bag. "Just like a proper southern lady should."

"Are you the new attendant?" her Grandmother asked, looking at Alexis.

"Oh, she's been bad lately," Mabel shared, lowering her voice. "Doesn't know me half the time." The women watched Mary as she sat in the chair smiling. "She does seem happy, though!" They looked at each other, and shared a weak smile.

"Thank goodness for that." Alexis unlocked the brakes on the wheel chair and pushed her Grandmother toward the door.

"We do have that." Mabel nodded her head in agreement and opened the door as they made their way into the hall.

"We're good to go, Mabel. I'll take it from here," Alexis said as she continued to push the chair down the hallway and toward the dining room.

"You have a nice dinner now. I'll check on you shortly," Mabel commented as she stepped out of the room and closed the door.

"Thank you Mabel." Alexis waved and continued to push her Grandmother down the long hall until they reached wide double doors that opened into a spacious, but cozy dining room. She looked around the empty space and selected a small table where she parked her Grandmother.

"It looks like we got here early!" Alexis commented.

"Ladies?" A server soon greeted them. "Did you get a chance to look at today's menu?"

"Oh, June, we don't need to look. My Grandmother will have whatever chicken dish that's available with broccoli. She loves her chicken and broccoli," Alexis squeezed her Grandma's hand. "I'll just take a plate full of whatever vegetables you're serving today and a side of rice."

"We can certainly do that," June said as she poured water in the glasses placed before the women. "I won't be long." She quickly left and headed to the kitchen to place the orders.

Alexis sat in silence with her Grandmother as music softly played over a speaker system. The room was filled with tables spaced out to accommodate the many wheelchairs that visited daily. One wall was lined with large windows that overlooked acres of fields and woods. The room was nicely decorated with neutral colors and tables were covered with white linens. Alexis remembered how relieved she was when she first visited and saw that the dining area did not resemble a cafeteria, but felt more like a nicely appointed restaurant. Situated in the country, the facilities offered lower costs and high quality. Mary Bradford, once an active mother, gardener, grand dame of fine southern social gatherings, and the wise advisor to a young Alexis was now on her own, with a limited social circle not of her choosing. It was important to find her a home that held to her high standards of class and refinement.

Dax Bradford was fifteen years older than Mary and made it to the ripe age of 98 before his body gave out. He was a caring and kind husband, although sometimes a rigid and stubborn man. A home body, he was always tinkering in the workshop in the back of the house and could fix just about anything. Dax ruled the roost and Mary abided by his rules. The laundry had to be done on a certain day, the meals served at specific times, and the dutiful wife complied, was grateful, and never complained. Their love was strong and she understood him and in the end, she always had the last say. He respected her and made sure all her needs were met. Now she was alone and free to live life on her terms, but at age 88 and suffering from dementia, her dream of travel to foreign lands was never going to be realized. Even fancy ladies' luncheons were a fading memory.

It was only a few years later that Alexis would be alone, her parents gone from unexpected separate illnesses. With no one to help care for her, she knew that it was time to place her Grandmother in Assisted Living where she would receive needed attention. It was not an easy decision. They were all they had, each other, and Alexis would do anything for her Gran who had always been there for her.

Dementia had set in, and the decision was inevitable. Mary was no longer fully aware and never felt the loss of leaving her home of over 50 years with Dax. Her garden, now overgrown, was too much work and filled in by the new homeowners. Alexis never told her Gran, not that she would have understood. Her new view was the rolling fields filled with tall weeds and wildflowers behind the Creekside home with Georgia mountains as a backdrop. Yes, the dementia brought an ease to her aging Grandmother and she was fortunate to see the world through a filter that was sometimes magical. It was this view that brought peace to Alexis who couldn't initially bear the complexity of the situation. For now, it worked.

Residents were slowly filtering in and making their way to surrounding tables for their early dinners. Alexis recognized many, greeted them and made small talk when she saw Mabel enter the room wheeling an elderly man to a nearby table. Following them was a tall, handsome man in his 30's, his hair slightly long, wearing a sweater and jeans. He thanked Mabel who chatted for a while as she situated them.

Mabel turned and spotted Alexis and Mary, waved, and approached their table. "Are you two Okay over here? Did you order yet?" she asked.

"We did, thank you." Alexis watched the attractive man who was engaged in conversation with the elderly gentlemen. The men laughed loudly, bringing a smile to Alexis's face.

Mabel grinned as she watched Alexis notice the new arrivals. "He's a mighty handsome man, don't you think?" she asked, observing Alexis and her obvious curiosity.

Alexis suddenly realized that Mabel noticed her staring and broke her gaze, clearing her throat. "Ah hem!" she feigned a cough. "Who?" Alexis coughed once again.

"The gentlemen that I just escorted in. I thought perhaps you noticed." Mabel continued to smile at Alexis's girlish behavior.

"Oh, the two men that you seated. No, I wasn't paying attention, actually. I guess they would be new here?" she asked.

"That's Mr. Winters and his Grandson Colton. Mr. Winters moved in recently and Mr. Colton is checking out the place. I hope they're on their game in the kitchen!" Mabel's eyes widened.

"I'm sure they'll live up to expectations." Alexis glanced up, trying to act discrete.

"He sure is a handsome man, don't you think Miss Alexis?" Mabel asked again, raising an eyebrow.

"Oh, I didn't really notice." Alexis fidgeted with her napkin and looked down at her lap. "His hair is a little long," she said without looking up.

"I think it's nice. Looks a little like one of those warrior characters, like, like, what's that Swedish warrior?" she asked.

"You mean Thor?" Alexis asked.

"Yes Ma'am! Thor! Isn't that the name of that good lookin' Viking kind of character you see on the cover of romance novels?" Mabel became excited. "You'd know Miss Alexis, being a fiction writer and all! Isn't that the character?"

"Yes, Mabel. That's the character. Thor is actually a Nordic God and I can't recall seeing him on the cover of any novels," Alexis grinned, shooting another quick glance at the stranger.

"Well, *I* think he's handsome," Mary piped in.

"Grandma! Why you little cougar," Alexis teased, finding herself caught off guard at the humorous comment.

"I don't know what a cougar is, but I was talking about the one in the wheelchair," Mary responded still watching the newcomers. The elderly man looked over at the three women as though aware of the conversation and connected eyes with Mary. The two smiled.

"I'd be happy to take you over there to meet him," Mabel offered.

"Oh no, Mabel! Absolutely not! We wouldn't want to interrupt their dinner. Besides, we ordered already and I'm sure our food will be coming soon," Alexis argued, still fidgeting in her seat.

"Don't be silly, Alexis. Dinner can wait. I want to meet my new neighbor," Mary said as she attempted to move her wheelchair, reaching down to unlock the brakes.

"Woah there tiger, I'll take care of that." Mabel stepped over and took charge, unlocking the wheels and pulled the chair away from the table. Alexis rolled her eyes, realizing that she had been out voted.

"I like tiger. I don't like cougar. I'm a tiger," Mary pulled her shawl tightly around her shoulders, sat straight in her chair and proudly smiled.

"She picks now to be funny!" Alexis stood, taking a posture of obvious reluctance and then defeat. "Well tiger, let's go on over there and meet Mr. Winters and his son." Mabel winked at Alexis who managed a smile.

"Now that's more like it. No harm in that," Mabel nodded her head as she slowly pushed the wheelchair forward and across the room. "Mr. Winters," Mabel said as she approached the table where the two gentlemen were now reviewing their menus.

"Which one?" the younger man asked as he stood.

"Why the distinguished gentleman," Mary answered, smiling at the elderly man in the wheelchair.

"I'm so sorry to interrupt your dinner, but my Grandmother insisted," Alexis began to apologize.

"There's no need to apologize," the handsome man answered as he extended his hand to Alexis. "We were hoping to meet residents and families. I'm Colton and this is Gus Winters, my Grandfather. It's a pleasure to meet both of you."

"And who is this young, charming woman," the elderly man asked as he extended his hand to Mary whose wheelchair was now parked next to his.

"Mary. Mary Bradford." Mary extended her hand with a look of confidence and authority when Mr. Winters suddenly, but gently kissed it, prompting a loud giggle from her.

"Well, Mary Bradford, it's a pleasure to meet you." Mr. Winters gave her a warm smile and patted her hand before returning it. Mary giggled once again.

"Oh, you charming man!" She grinned and batted her eyelashes.

Alexis nervously cleared her throat, disrupting the sweet scene. "So, you're new to Creekside?" she asked, directing her question to the elderly Mr. Winters who continued to stare at Mary.

"Yes," Colton answered for him. "He just arrived," he said as he stood and walked to the other side of the table and pulled out a chair for Alexis. Mabel quickly took the cue and secured Mary's wheelchair next to Mr. Winters. "Please, join us, won't you?" Colton gestured at the empty chair, as all waited for her answer.

"Oh no, we," Alexis began. "We really couldn't. Our dinner is coming out shortly and Gran, you know how you like your dinner nice and hot."

"We would love to!" Mary stated. "So, Mr. Winters," she began as she turned toward him, completely engaged in his presence.

"Oh, please call me Gus. And may I call you Mary?" Mr. Winters politely asked.

"Mary or FiFi. Whatever you'd like," she smiled.

"Gran? Who is FiFi? Your name is Mary," Alexis gently reminded her. "I'm sorry," Alexis whispered to Colton before taking her seat, "my Grandmother has dementia and I never know what she might say. We may hear some *interesting* comments and I apologize in advance."

"I think she's charming," Colton loudly stated as he smiled and pushed Alexis's chair in, giving it an extra push.

"FiFi? I like FiFi," Mr. Winters laughed. "You know I've always wanted to be Harry. My full name is Gustav. Gus, for short. Gus is a good name, but Harry has character, you know?"

"Yes, I understand. Mary is nice, but FiFi, well, we never know what ol' FiFi will be up to!" Mary winked.

"Then FiFi it is," Mr. Winters announced and patted Mary's hand.

"Oh Lord," Alexis spouted under her breath putting her head in her hands, shaking it in disbelief.

"FiFi and Harry! I like it," Mr. Winters bellowed as he and Mary laughed loudly.

"I haven't seen your Grandmother blush like that, well, ever!" Mabel said as she leaned next to Alexis, lowering her voice. She then turned toward Mary and Mr. Winters. "Miss Mary, I'll leave you in the hands of your Granddaughter. Now you behave! I'll check back with you in a while," Mabel paused, "I mean FiFi." She laughed out loud and quickly walked to a nearby table, greeted and chatted with the guests.

Mary and Mr. Winters immediately became deeply immersed in conversation, laughing and sharing stories, oblivious to the presence of their Grandchildren.

"I grew up on a farm, Harry," Mary shared as they quickly launched into a discussion of their pasts.

"I'm a big fan of farming myself. Had my own farm, in fact. Flew planes and did a bit of crop dusting in my day," Mr. Winters shared.

"A pilot! That *is* impressive!" Mary looked intrigued and leaned in closer to Mr. Winters, then whispered something in his ear that prompted them both to laugh loudly.

"It looks like Harry's made a new friend," Colton smiled as he leaned in closer to Alexis.

"I am *so* sorry about this," she apologized once again.

"You apologize a lot, don't you?" He cocked his head to one side examining her face closely. Alexis nervously pushed her chair in closer to the table. "I never did get your name," he continued.

"Oh, I'm sorry, I mean it's Alexis," she laughed.

"Alexis, nice to meet you. Has your Grandmother been here long?" he asked as he watched Mary happily flirt with his Grandfather.

"A few years. It started when she broke her hip and then the dementia seemed to get worse after we moved her here. I think she started to give up, you know?" Alexis watched her Grandmother and smiled. "Mabel mentioned that your Grandfather just moved in."

"Just a couple of days ago. He's had arthritis and back issues. He's totally of sound mind, but it's just too difficult for him to get around on his own. We've been taking care of him ourselves, but he'll get much more attention here not to mention the daily therapy. We live in a fairly remote area which makes it tough to get him proper medical care."

"We?" Alexis turned her head to one side and caught herself, embarrassed at the inquiry. "Oh, I'm sorry. I don't mean to pry!"

"Again with the apologies," Colton smiled. "Yes, *we*. My Dad and I. We lost my Mother years ago. It's just the two of us and of course Harry over there," he teased, prompting a smile from Alexis. "That's better," Colton said as he turned toward her.

"Seriously I don't know what that was all about," Alexis watched as Mary and Gus chatted away. Colton raised his eyebrows. "I mean the FiFi thing. She can be unpredictable."

"Fun. It's about fun. Does it matter if it's the dementia or not? It's good to be silly don't you think?" Colton asked.

"I guess so. It's been a very long time since I've been silly. Besides, I'm not sure that was my Grandmother's intention. She can just go off on some pretty strange tangents which may or may not be dementia." She paused, wondering just how much she should share with this stranger, then leaned forward. "She talks to Archangel Michael. She thinks he hangs in her room and has conversations with her."

"Oh really? Then my Grand Dad is in the right place. If Michael's hanging out here, then I know he'll be in good hands," Colton grinned. "Seriously, I think your Grandmother is just having a good time. I'm glad that my Grand Dad has a friend. I feel much better knowing that he won't be sitting in that room alone when I'm not here. This is a tough transition for us all, but I know that it's the right decision. It's just difficult. He was always the leader, the strong one."

"I know. My Grandmother was smart as a whip, feisty, and the wise one that I could count on. It's never easy, but they have the best care now. I think that you'll be pleased with the staff. I know it's not home, but I think that Harry over there will be happy with the quality of the facilities. The food is pretty good, too." Alexis watched her Grandmother chatting away. "I have to say that I haven't seen my gran quite so engaged in a very long time. I'm sure that she's having more fun with your Grandfather than listening to me read to her."

"Oh, you read to her? My Grand Dad is a big reader. Maybe he can read to her." Mary's and Alexis's dinners arrived at their table.

"Oh, hey, our dinners have arrived. I'm going to take my Gran back to our table and give you some time alone with your Grandfather." Alexis stood and prepared to wheel Mary back.

"You're welcome to stay," Colton offered.

"I appreciate the offer, but your Grandfather and my Grandmother will get to spend plenty of time together. It's important for family to have quality visits, especially when they first arrive. Besides, you have a long drive so I know you'll want to spend as much time with him as possible." Alexis pulled the brakes off Mary's chair. "Gran, we're going to let Mr. Winters and his Grandson have their dinner. You'll get to see Mr. Winters soon." She pulled the chair away from the table as Colton stood.

"Okay," Mary said and extended her hand. Mr. Winters kissed it again. "Harry, you *are* a charmer!"

"FiFi, you aren't so bad yourself," he teased.

Alexis turned toward Colton and extended her hand. "Colton, it was a real pleasure."

"I hope we'll . . . *I'll* see you again soon," Colton said as he shook her hand, looking as though he had more to say.

"Of course. I'm sure we will. Thank you, and thank you Mr. Winters for charming my Gran! It was a pleasure meeting you. I hope that you settle in nicely at Creekside. I know that you'll enjoy it here." Alexis smiled and wheeled Mary back to their table as Mr. Winters gave her a wave.

Alexis situated her Grandmother, placing a napkin on her lap before taking her own seat. "I'm sorry, Gran, but Mr. Winters just arrived and I didn't want to take up his time when his Grandson was visiting." Alexis placed her hand on top of Mary's.

"Oh, I don't mind," Mary smiled and patted Alexis's hand.

"You don't?" Alexis asked with a look of confusion.

"No. Harry asked me out on a date. I'll be seeing him soon. I understand." Mary patted Alexis's hand again and then pulled it away to pick up her fork as she began to eat.

"You have a date?" Alexis stared at her Grandmother.

"You can close your mouth, Alexis. It's not all *that* shocking." Mary took a large bite of broccoli and smiled as she chewed.

"Wow." Alexis slowly picked up her fork and poked at her vegetables. "Good for you, Gran." She looked up at her Grandmother, shook her head and smiled. "My Gran has a date. Huh!" she laughed. Her Grandmother joined in her laughter, revealing a mouth full of food, prompting an even louder laugh from Alexis.

⁂

"Well hello." Miss Alexis looked up to see a tall, silver haired man standing before her. "It's a bit chilly out here, don't you think Dear?" the man asked.

The elderly woman laughed and extended her hand. He took it in his and placed his other hand over hers. "Not too bad for December," she replied with a smile. "You know I'm not one to let the cold stop me from enjoying the garden."

"May I?" The man motioned to a patio chair next to her.

"Of course," she gestured for him to sit down, carefully examined his face and smiled. "I was prepared for visitors. It's good to see you."

"It's always good to see you, my Dear." He moved the chair closer and took a seat. "Enjoying a nice glass of wine, I see," he pointed to the glass that she held.

"One awaits you, tucked in the bag." She raised her glass and smiled, then took a sip.

The tall man flashed a big smile, stood and walked to the back of her wheel chair, removing the black bag. He unzipped it and took out a glass along with the bottle of wine, pouring some in his and splashing a bit more in hers before securing the top and placing it back in the bag.

"Oh!" she laughed. "It's a good thing I'm not driving!"

He expertly swirled the ruby liquid, then stuck his nose in and took a long, satisfying sniff. One hand in his pocket, the other swirling the wine, he gazed over the acres of fields and gardens with a look of satisfaction before sitting down. He crossed his leg over the other and rested his arm on his knee as he leaned back and relaxed. Taking another sip of wine, he let out a deep breath and closed his eyes.

"Ahhh yes, a good year indeed." He took a second sip and held it in his mouth, swished it around for a moment, then swallowed.

"How have you been?" Miss Alexis asked.

"Never better, my Dear. Never better." He nodded. "Except for not spending more time with you, of course."

She looked out over the garden, taking in a deep breath then slowly exhaling. "Ah, I can smell the garden, even in its dormant state. It's so fresh." She turned and looked him directly in the eyes. "I'm sorry that you haven't been able to join me out here lately." She watched for his reaction.

"I've been out here a few times on my own. I visited you in your room several times, but you were asleep and I didn't want to disturb you. I know that you haven't been well," he answered.

"Getting old my Dear, getting old." She gave a slight smile. "I'm just so tired. Things wear out!" She shrugged her shoulders. "I got my second wind today and decided that I would view the gardens and enjoy a glass of wine!"

"Yes, here we are, right where we started," he laughed.

"Yes," she smiled and grinned at him. "Right where it all began. We've come full circle, haven't we?"

"We certainly have," he smiled and paused. "I'm sorry that I haven't visited you more often," he apologized.

"It's fine, my dear. I understand. You have other things to tend to. I'm just glad that you were able to come today while I'm out here and not confined to that bed," she stated.

"Where's Annabel?" he asked.

"Oh, I forgot my Christmas charm," Miss Alexis answered. "She went back in to retrieve it."

They both sat in silence for a moment. "I want you to know," he began and paused, "I want you to know that you have always meant so much to me." He watched Miss Alexis for a response.

She looked out over the garden and took a sip, slightly nodding her head. "I was just reminiscing about the first time we met, here at Creekside. We've always been the best of friends, haven't we?" She looked at him and smiled. "Above all else."

"Yes." He reached over and took her hand in his. "Yes, indeed. It's been a long journey, but we've always remained the best of friends. Thank you for that." They sat in silence, enjoying the beauty of the garden. A slight breeze rustled the patches of tall, dried field grass, making a calming, swooshing sound.

Chapter Three

"Hello!" Jill stuck her head in the front door. "May I enter?"

"Come on in, neighbor," Alexis said as she sat at her computer, once again in her pajamas. "What brings you here?"

Jill walked into the dining room, folded her arms and sighed. "Just as I thought."

"What?" Alexis asked.

"Again with the pajamas! At least you've changed them. That's a good sign," Jill teased.

"Well look at you all dressed up. Next to you, yes, I'm not dressed appropriately! But I have to ask; if I was sitting here in a sweat suit would that be better?" Alexis asked, planting her elbows on the table and placing her face in her hands as she stared at Jill and batted her eyelashes.

"Hmmm. Let me think about that. Sweat suit versus pajamas." Jill looked off into space and paused, placed her finger on her lips and tapped. "Yep. I vote for the sweat suit."

"You're just saying that based on if we were in public, but I'm in my own home. They're simply more comfortable and they're nice and warm. That's all. It doesn't *mean* anything! Besides, I'm a writer and, well, writers are quirky."

"Writers are quirky? Oh girlfriend, that's not happening," Jill unfolded her arms and stared at Alexis.

"What do you mean that's not happening?" Alexis casually sat back in her chair.

"I think that I need a vote on this one," Jill smirked.

"A vote? There are two of us and I'm sorry to tell you, but it's a stale mate." Alexis thought for a moment. "Wait, it's my home so I get two votes! Orange Kitty gets one too! Yep, three votes to one. I win!" Alexis gave a proud look, but Jill was unaffected. "Hello? Are you with me here?"

"I disagree. I think I'm holding more votes," Jill responded.

"I'm not following you," Alexis looked confused. "I think you may be delusional, my friend."

"Yep. It's time to vote on whether it's quirky and cool for a writer to sit and work in her pajamas every day!" Jill smiled cleverly.

"Well, unless Willow and Orange Kitty are voting on your side, I would have to disagree with you," Alexis said. "It's totally cool to hang in my PJ's."

Jill walked to the front door and opened it. "Girls, I could use your opinion on something." Alexis's friends Pamela and Faye appeared.

"Oh no." Alexis stuck her head in her hands, and hid her face.

"Oh yes," Pamela responded as she walked in the door and stood in front of Alexis, examining her. "We're here for the party, but unfortunately, it's not a pajama party!"

Faye looked closely at Alexis who still had her face buried in her hands. "Honey, are you crying?"

Alexis's shoulders began to rhythmically move up and down.

"Oh, honey! It's Okay! We're not here to judge you!" Pamela placed her arms around Alexis and Faye joined her in a group hug. "We just wanted to help!"

"See?" Faye looked at Jill with a concerned expression. "We upset her. I told you this was a bad idea."

Alexis raised her head revealing tears that rolled down her face. She grabbed a tissue from the box, still poised next to her computer. "No, it's Okay. Jill's right. I've been a little depressed and I have to admit that I'm embarrassed. Look at me! I'm even shopping in my PJ's!"

"What? You went shopping in your PJs?" Faye looked at Jill.

"Don't ask," Jill shook her head. "At least she gets dressed up to see her Gran. That's a start."

"Alexis," Faye leaned over and kissed the top of her head. "I know it's been a rough two years losing your Mom and Dad so close together."

Alexis sniffled, "and Skuttlebutt."

"And Skuttlebutt. We all loved the little guy too, but you can't hide behind your computer, Alexis." Faye looked at the other women who joined in a supportive smile.

"I know, but it's what I do for a living!" Alexis objected.

Faye, stood and looked around the living room. "Did you put up another Christmas tree?" She asked as she examined several trees in various places.

"Yeah." Alexis wiped her eyes with a tissue. "There are smaller ones in the other rooms." She sniffled.

"It's a bit early but they're beautiful," Pamela said, staring in amazement at the perfectly decorated trees.

"Pamela! Focus!" Jill snapped her fingers.

"Right." Pamela stood in attention, before turning back to the purpose of their surprise appearance. "Alexis, we know what you do for a living which is why it's even that much more important to force yourself to interact with the outside world. So, we're here to do an intervention." Pamela announced.

"Well, I guessed that already," Alexis said rolling her eyes.

"We're here to get you out of those pajamas and out of this house, even if it's for one night," Pamela walked behind Alexis, placing her hands on her shoulders as though anticipating an attempted escape. "You may get up now, go up those stairs and pick out something pretty to wear. A dress would be nice. We're going to a wine tasting."

"Now? You want to go out now?" Alexis's jaw dropped as she turned around and stared intently at Pamela.

"Yes, *now*! Don't think we're going to back down. Go up there and get ready because this isn't an optional outing," Faye chimed in. "We already purchased your ticket and you're going!"

"Jill!" Alexis looked to Jill for support.

"Oh girlfriend, don't look to me to get you out of this. We've been planning this for quite some time and when this wine tasting came up, we thought it'd be the perfect opportunity. You love wine and you used to love these types of events. Come on! It'll be fun."

"Used to. *Used* to love them. Obviously, you're not asking me, you're telling me." Alexis stood, looked at her three friends and let out a long sigh. "I'll go, but I'm driving separately!"

"Oh no you're not," Faye quickly responded. "You're going to have some wine like the rest of us, so we're taking a taxi. You aren't getting out of this that easily!"

Alexis sighed once again and slowly shuffled to the bottom of her staircase where she paused. "What if we just went out to a restaurant or something?" she suggested as Jill motioned her up the stairs. Alexis shook her head and slowly shuffled up each step. Pamela pointed to Jill, indicating that she should follow Alexis.

"Make sure it's something sexy," Pamela ordered.

Alexis grudgingly made her way into her Master bathroom and pulled out a makeup kit, curling iron, and toothbrush. "You'll be happy to know that I already showered!" she shouted to Jill who was now rifling through Alexis's closet.

"Good, because we don't have much time before it starts." Jill continued to push through the hangers, occasionally examining an outfit. "This is cute," she pulled out a dress and held it high before sorting through more. "Oh, and here's another cute dress. How about this one!" She carefully laid a stack of dresses on the bed in a neat display.

"I don't care," Alexis shouted from the bathroom. "You choose!"

"This is fun!" Jill examined the collection and picked up a bright, red dress. She then opened a small closet lined with shoes. Each pair was perfectly placed as though part of a department store display. "When was the last time you put on a pair of heels?"

Alexis stuck her head out of the bathroom door, her toothbrush hanging from her mouth. She shrugged her shoulders.

Jill examined each shelf, her finger running across the edge until she stopped at a pair of black, strappy suede stilettos. "Oh, yes! Here's the ticket!" She grabbed the pair, holding them next to the bright red dress.

"Unt er thick isha bish mush!" Alexis mumbled as she pushed the toothbrush around her mouth, toothpaste foaming on her lips.

"You think this is a bit much? Heck no! Everyone is going to be wearing little black dresses. But you! You will be the bell of the ball in your little 'red' dress." Jill pushed the dress and shoes toward Alexis. "Put it on. You'll look great!"

Alexis took the dress and shoes, placing them on a bench in the bathroom before rinsing her mouth. "Don't you think this dress is a bit tight? I mean this is a wine tasting, Jill," she complained.

"No, it's not too tight. You have a great figure. Show it off, Alexis! Now speed it up, will you?" Jill ordered.

Alexis looked in the mirror, pulling at her face as she lifted her cheeks with her fingers. "Oh boy," she sighed. "I'm too old for this!" she shouted out to Jill, and began to apply a coat of foundation with a brush. Freckles and imperfections disappeared and with another stroke, rosy cheeks now brightened her pale face. Mascara, a bit of eyeshadow and lipstick and Alexis began to recognize the vibrant woman that she once was. She felt a brief flush of excitement and quickly slipped into the red dress. Did she buy that for a Christmas party last year? She couldn't remember. It had been quite some time since she had worn a cocktail dress and it didn't matter. It still fit perfectly. She slipped on the suede high heels, laced up the straps and examined herself in the mirror before making her entrance.

"Oh!" Jill exclaimed. "Perfection!" She stood up and hugged Alexis. "I'm so proud of you and I don't want to hear about how *old* you are! You are a young, intelligent woman in her prime!"

"Who hasn't been out since forever. I can't remember the last time I wore these," Alexis looked down at her feet, her ankles wavering. "I'll be lucky if I can walk in them."

"That won't matter. We'll be standing most of the time. You just need to look good and taste wines." Jill grabbed her hand. "Come on. Let's go down and show the girls."

Alexis wobbled behind Jill as they made their way down the stairs and into the living room where Faye and Pamela sat, patiently waiting.

"You look gorgeous!" Faye exclaimed.

"I tried to find my flannel cocktail dress, but it must be at the cleaners," Alexis responded as she managed a smile.

"Well, you look lovely!" Pamela stood and hugged Alexis.

"Okay, Okay, and just for the record, I don't wear my pajamas all day, every day. Just once in a while. Can we please not make a big deal out of this?" Alexis said acting somewhat embarrassed. She walked to the hallway closet and pulled out her coat.

"Girls, the car is pulling up. Let's get this show on the road!" Faye announced as she hung up her cell phone and placed it back in her purse. The four women made their way outside the brick bungalow where the taxi appeared.

"Wait!" Alexis turned and looked at the house. "What about Orange Kitty?"

"Oh for crying out loud, Alexis, haven't you given that poor cat a name yet?" Pamela asked.

"Yeah, Orange Kitty. He's not my cat. He's a stray and what's wrong with that name? He comes to it." Alexis frowned.

"Accept it, Alexis. He may have started out as a stray, but he's your cat now. And you're a writer. You're more creative than that. Orange Kitty isn't a name," Pamela said as she climbed into the back seat of the taxi.

"It most certainly is," Alexis argued. "If celebrities can name their kids Apple and Jet, I can name my stray cat Orange Kitty!"

"Good point," Pamela laughed. "He'll be fine. You'll be back early enough. He's a cat! They take care of themselves."

Alexis watched her home shrinking into the distance as the car pulled away. Dusk set in and soft outdoor garden and holiday lights glowed on many neighborhood homes. It was a short ride to The Garden Tavern, a large English style restaurant and event location overlooking a beautiful city park. The four piled out of the taxi and made their way into the historic, stone building and checked in at a table set up in the large entrance.

"Welcome ladies. I just need to put these wrist bands on you. Wine glasses are over on that table. You can each grab one and join the event," a young woman instructed as she took their tickets and strapped green paper bands around each of their wrists. "Enjoy!"

The four chatted excitedly as they entered the event space which revealed a wall of windows that overlooked the park. Now dark and empty except for the occasional dog walker, a pathway that encircled the park was lit by elegant trees weaved with white, miniature lights.

"I haven't been here in ages," Alexis stated as the four stood and viewed the dozens of tables that lined the perimeter of the room. Each was filled with bottles of wine, and dump buckets. Behind them stood vintners, pouring and chatting with the guests who eagerly reached out their glasses for tastes.

"Divide and conquer," Faye announced.

"Divide? No one said anything about dividing!" Alexis objected.

"It's the only way we'll get you to meet new people. Otherwise, we might as well be sitting in your living room with a bottle of wine!" Jill said.

"You guys are tough!" Alexis frowned.

"Don't worry. It's just to get you over being uncomfortable and withdrawn. We promise that we'll come find you shortly," Pamela assured her.

"You'd better mean that! Promise?" Alexis said as she nervously looked around the room. "And I'm not uncomfortable and withdrawn!"

"Of course, you aren't. Don't worry, you can easily find us, Alexis! The room isn't *that* big. I'm starting with the whites," Faye claimed.

"I guess I'll go over here to the Burgundy table," Alexis reluctantly declared. "Now don't go far, girls." She paused. "Seriously, can't we just walk around together?"

"We'll check in on occasion," Pamela smiled, taking Alexis by the shoulders and giving her a soft nudge. "Then we'll reconvene. We *will*, Alexis. Now go!"

"This is so weird!" Alexis slowly walked toward the first table, taking her place in a short line of attendees.

"Hi," she said as she reached the table and smiled at the pourer who watched her examine the various bottles. "What do we have here?"

"You look lost. What if we start you off with the first one and work our way down the line," he suggested as he raised a bottle.

Alexis smiled. "I guess you're right, I just need to get started."

"That's what you're here for!" he smiled as he lifted a bottle and splashed wine into her glass. She carefully tasted the pour, gently swishing it around her mouth, stepping aside to let others in.

"Not doing it for you?" the vintner asked.

"It's nice, but a bit sharp. Do you have anything smoother?" she asked.

"Well, let's see," he said as he moved to the next bottle. "Try this." He splashed the second wine in her glass.

Alexis concentrated on the flavors before emptying the rest of the contents in the dump bucket. Once again, the vintner poured another taste, explaining its origins. Once again, she tasted and discarded it before thanking him and moving to the next table.

"My taste buds must be off tonight," she said to the woman standing behind the next selection of wines.

"Not finding anything that appeals to you?" she asked. "What kind of wine do you usually like?"

"I guess more of a full-bodied red. I usually drink Burgundy, but

I see that there are mostly American wineries here." Alexis picked up a bottle and examined it.

"Perhaps a Pinot Noir would do the trick," said a man standing directly behind her. Alexis turned to see Colton, wine glass in hand and a big smile.

"Colton! What are you doing here? I thought that you lived in northern country!" she stated, trying to hide her delight.

"I do! But, I had business after I got Grand Dad settled in and stayed in town. So, here I am!" He continued to smile, showing his perfect teeth. "What a pleasure to see you!"

"This certainly is a surprise and an incredible coincidence!" Alexis said, stunned at the odds of running into him.

"Well, just to set the record straight, I'm not stalking you," he teased.

"Oh, I didn't mean," Alexis paused and laughed. "Of course you aren't. So, how is your Grandfather settling in?" she asked, trying to act casual.

"So far, he's pretty happy. He talked more about your Grandmother than he did anything else. She made quite an impression on him."

"Oh really? Well, she was a spitfire in her day and your Grandfather seems to have ignited that spirit. My Grandfather's been gone for several years, so I know she must appreciate the male companionship," Alexis shared.

"I believe that Harry and FiFi are going to be good friends." They both laughed, then stood for a few moments in an awkward silence. Colton walked to the wine table, and picked up a bottle. "Is this what you're drinking?"

"Yeah, but nothing seems to be doing the trick," she shared, looking at her empty glass.

"Come with me. I think I know where we can find a wine that may be more to your liking." Colton pointed to the other side of the room. "Shall we?" He offered his arm.

"Sure," Alexis replied. "Maybe I'll have better luck. We're here to explore, right?" she said as she gently took his arm.

"Right!" Colton agreed as he escorted her to a table filled with local wines.

"*Georgia* wines?" Alexis wrinkled her nose.

"Ah, I see some hesitation! A bit of wine snobbery perhaps?" he smiled, raising his eyebrows.

"Well," she paused. "I have to admit that I am a bit of a Burgundy snob. If we're being totally honest here, the answer would be 'yes,'" she admitted.

Colton greeted the pourer behind the table. "May I?" he asked as he picked up a bottle. The pourer nodded in approval. "Swish your glass out with water and let's give this a try." Colton poured water in her glass and Alexis humored him by swirling and dumping it in a bucket before accepting a small taste of the wine.

"Go ahead and take a good sniff." Colton poured some in his own glass, swirled and stuck his nose in. "Ah, that is a beauty!" He took a sip and held it in his mouth, swishing it around.

Alexis, still sniffing, watched Colton. "Is that what I'm supposed to be doing?"

Colton smiled. "If you'd like. It distributes the full taste to every part of your tongue."

Alexis took a deep breath, sipped and swished her wine. "Nice. I liked that!" She held her glass out for another pour.

"Nice, right? It's a Pinot Noir. Clean, but bold and intense with a hint of blackberry and pepper," he said as he poured her another taste.

Alexis swirled the wine and sipped it again. "Yeah. Pepper. I never thought of pepper, but that's exactly what I'm tasting. And I love the blackberry. It's not too heavy."

"That's why I like it so much. It's a lighter red, but still holds a bold taste." Colton took another sip as he carefully watched Alexis. "You have a good pallet."

She looked at him with a grin. "Thanks. It's a good wine." She paused. "So, you're a wine connoisseur?"

"You could say that," he smiled and raised his glass to the pourer behind the table. "She likes it!" he said to the man who gave two thumbs up.

"Are these available for purchase today?" Alexis walked to the table and picked up one of the bottles.

"Yes, Ma'am. All of these wines are available. We have some here, or I can order them for pickup or delivery. Or you could visit the winery. We have tastings on weekends with entertainment and we serve some nice dishes from local suppliers. It's pretty special," the attendant explained and winked at Colton.

"Oh, my gosh," Alexis stared at the bottle which was wrapped in a beautiful, silver label with snow covered trees. She read the print. "Winters Winery?" she stated out loud as she looked at Colton. "That can't be a coincidence! Winters? As in,"

"As in Gustav . . . better known as Gus, Carl and Colton Winters. Yes." He grinned as he looked up from his glass. "And let's not forget Gus's alter ego, 'Harry,'" he laughed.

"Seriously?" She looked at the pourer who nodded his head in agreement. "This is the business you stayed for? This is *your* winery?"

"Well, not mine exactly. My Great Grandfather started it, and then Grand Dad continued the legacy and expanded on it. My Dad was trained. They trained me and I eventually joined in the operations. Great Grand Dad was originally a wood worker and had a mill. It was on a pretty big piece of property and he decided to use the rest of the land to grow grapes. I know that may seem odd, but he enjoyed wines. He really got into it and being at the base of the Blue Ridge offered a good climate. So, why not, right?"

"Why not indeed! This is amazing." Alexis examined the other bottles on the table.

"Would you like to try another?" the pourer asked. Alexis nodded as he raised a bottle and showed it to Colton who gave a look of approval.

"That one won an award up against some tough California and European competition," Colton beamed with pride.

"No kidding!" Feeling confident, Alexis took her time, swirling the wine before sifting it through her teeth and over her tongue. "Very nice," she nodded her head. "I'm impressed." Alexis now looked at him with new interest.

Colton watched in amusement as she examined each of the wine bottles.

"That one," Colton said as he pointed, "is one of the first wines my Grand Dad perfected. It's our signature wine." He lifted the bottle and poured. "It's my favorite."

"Colton, you've completely changed my mind about local wines." Alexis lifted her glass and looked at the color against the light and discretely watched him as he turned and poured a taste for several patrons. He seemed taller and even more handsome than the first time they met. His longer hair now seemed sexy and not out of place as she first thought.

She felt her face flush. "So, your Great Grand Dad was a wood worker. Is that something your family continued?"

"Yeah. It's a passion of ours. My Dad and I work together at the shop, making furniture and custom pieces."

"Interesting. Wine and wood working. Is the business near the vineyards?" Alexis asked.

"It is. It's on the property. You should come visit the winery and I'll take you on a tour," Colton offered.

"Where are the Vineyards?" Alexis asked, finding herself more relaxed as the glow of the wine kicked in.

"At the base of the Blue Ridge. Tranquil River," he shared.

"I know Tranquil River. I just built a mountain home near there, in Peaceful Cove. Alexis paused and thought. "You know, I'm completing the interior of my mountain home and I need a mantel and some other natural furnishings. I'll take you up on the tour of the woodshop. Do you sell pieces there?"

"We do. We custom build, but we have many pieces at the shop," he replied.

"Then I believe a visit is in order," Alexis said as she picked up a napkin.

"Well then it's a date," Colton said as he poured for several more guests. He turned back to Alexis and caught her watching him closely, looking nervous. "Don't take the 'date' comment too seriously, Alexis." He grinned.

"It's not that. I just can't get over seeing you here. This is quite a coincidence don't you think?" she asked.

"Is it?" Colton asked with a smile.

"You don't think that *I*," Alexis straightened up.

"No! I didn't mean that you were stalking me!" Colton let out a big laugh.

"Whew! I thought maybe you thought I was some sort of nut! My girlfriends actually dragged me out." Alexis pointed to a table where Pamela and Faye stood, talking. "There they are. Loaded me in a taxi and here I am!" She waved at the girls who waved back with a look of curiosity. "So, are you saying that you think this is fate?" she asked.

"I do. Don't you?" Colton tilted his head to one side in anticipation of her answer.

"I don't know." She paused to think and looked out the window at the park below. "I suppose you're right. Nothing happens randomly." Alexis looked back at Colton. "It's funny, but I wouldn't have guessed you to be the kind of guy who believes in that sort of thing."

"Well, I guess you'll just have to get to know me then," he said as he picked up his glass and clinked it against hers.

"Since you believe in such things, what do you think it means?" she asked and took a sip.

"That, my girl, is the million-dollar question! I certainly think it's worth exploring further." Colton picked up the open bottle of Pinot Noir and handed it to Alexis. "Here. Take this over to your girlfriends and share. I'll also send you home with one. It's my insurance policy!" He gave her a wink as he handed her the bottle. "And just in case, take this." Colton handed her a business card. "The address of the vineyard and my phone number."

"Thanks. I guess I'll see you later." She slipped the card in her purse as Colton stepped behind the table and assisted in giving pours. "Oh, and thanks for the wine lesson!" she shouted as she walked away. Colton smiled and waved.

"What is this?" Faye asked as Alexis joined them, extending the bottle.

"Oh, just a wine that I like. One of the vintners sent me off with it so that I could share it with you. It's a Pinot Noir."

"Well, it looks like you like something else too. You were chatting with Mr. Gorgeous for quite some time!" Pamela chimed in.

"Don't deny it. We were watching!" Jill interrupted as she joined the three women. "He is *cute*! Is he really one of the vintners here?"

"Yes, Jill, he really is. Don't make a big deal out of it. I know him from Creekside, my Gran's elderly care home. He was there with his Grandfather and wanted to know what I thought of it," Alexis said pulling the cork out of the bottle. She held it out, waiting for glasses to be offered.

"Oh, I'll take a taste," Faye said gladly.

"Did he now?" Pamela gave Alexis a sly look.

"Yes. Yes, he did. He stayed in town for his wine tasting event and that's about as interesting as it gets." Alexis avoided eye contact. "Besides, he lives at the foothills of the Blue Ridge."

"Where the vineyards are! Isn't that right by your mountain home?" Pamela asked, also holding her glass out for wine.

"In the vicinity," Alexis poured her a taste, careful not to act too excited.

"*That's* convenient, don't you think?" Jill teased. "When are you going to see him again?"

"What makes you think that I'm going to see him again?" Alexis tried to look casual.

"Oh don't give me that dumb look. I saw him give you his business card. That man is interested in you, Alexis. You'd be a fool not to go out with him." Jill glanced over at Colton's table and carefully watched him mingle with the patrons.

"Sorry to disappoint you, but he didn't ask me out. I have a date with a fireplace mantel. He has a wood working shop and I happened to need a few things for the mountain house. He suggested that I come by for a tour and to check out some items."

"He has a wood working shop and he owns a vineyard? *And* he's gorgeous? That is one interesting guy. You're off to a good start girlfriend!" Jill took a sip of wine. "Oh, and it's *good* wine too!" She held her glass out. "More please!"

"It's a family business. His Great Grandfather was a wood worker and used their property to grow grapes." Alexis glanced back at Colton who was still busy pouring. He briefly looked up and caught her looking, smiled, and raised his glass. The four women raised their glasses, as Jill waved.

"Oh, Alexis, he's really cute! Who cares where he lives. Besides, you'll be spending more time at the mountain home, right?" Jill watched as Alexis casually sipped her wine.

"I guess. I'm really busy right now. I have a deadline with my novel," she responded with a sheepish look.

"Oh right," Pamela said, "you're too busy sitting around in your PJ's and feeding Orange Kitty. That's baloney and you know it. You have a computer and you can write anywhere. You don't even need an Internet connection to write your novel!"

"She has Internet at the mountain house," Faye reminded her.

"Hey, that was mean," Alexis frowned at Pamela.

"Sorry. It was meant to be! This is an intervention, remember? Don't think we forgot!" Pamela continued as she walked to another wine table. The girls followed.

"Geez, the girl sits in her pajamas all day and she isn't here five minutes and already has the hottest guy in the room asking her out!" Jill chimed in.

"Jill, seriously, I met him at the assisted living home," Alexis frowned as she poured more Pinot Noir from her private stash. "And, yes, I do have Internet in the mountains. You're right, I can write from there."

"By the way, make sure you say 'goodbye' to Handsome over there before we leave! It wouldn't hurt to remember your friends when you visit his vineyards, either," Pamela hinted.

"Pamela! She doesn't need us tagging along," Faye nudged her.

"Shoosh, Faye! Pamela's right. After all, we're the ones that got her out." Jill turned to Alexis. "Alexis, don't pay attention to Faye. If you want to bring your dear friends with you to Handsome's vineyards, then by all means, you do it!"

"His name is Colton," Alexis grinned. "Of course, I'll take you. Don't be silly. Now enough of Colton. May we continue our journey through wine country?"

"Agreed!" Jill looked around the room. "No more talk of Colton. Does he have any brothers?"

"Jill!" Alexis laughed. "You are relentless!"

"I'm not talking about Colton! I'm talking about his brother, or cousin, or whomever else in the family is single and looks like him!" Jill gave the girls a Cheshire grin. "Party poops!" she said as she pretended to pout before turning back to the wine table. "Oh, there's a nice one. May I have a taste?" Jill asked the server as she pushed her glass toward him.

Pamela nudged Alexis and leaned in. "This wasn't so bad, was it?"

Alexis shrugged her shoulders. "I guess not."

"You guess not!" Pamela pushed Alexis in a playful manner and the two laughed loudly.

"Yes! Alright! I admit that this *is* sort of fun," Alexis pushed her back, laughing.

"What are you two doing over there?" Faye asked. "Behave! We have some serious wine tasting to attend to."

The four continued to make their way around the room of tables, chatting and laughing. Alexis held tight to her bottle of Pinot Noir, sharing it with her friends until the event came to a close.

"I guess it's time," Alexis announced as she stood tall and took in a deep breath.

"Go get 'em girl!" Jill teased as she placed both hands on her shoulders.

"Jill, seriously?" Pamela said shaking her head in disapproval. "Give the girl some space."

"I'm not interfering!" Jill protested.

"Girls! It's Okay! I'm an adult. I can handle this. So, please excuse me while I say farewell to Colton and I'll meet you at the entrance." Alexis ordered.

"What? Can't we watch?" Jill asked.

Faye and Pamela placed their arms around Jill and escorted her out of the room as she continued to protest. Alexis laughed and took another breath before making her way to Colton's table.

"Hey there! You came back! See? It was the wine that did it. My insurance. Did your friends enjoy the tasting?" Colton asked as he placed bottles of wine in boxes.

"Yeah, all of us did. This was a nice event. And thanks for the Pinot Noir. My friends loved it. But, you don't have to give me a bottle. I'm more than happy to purchase it," Alexis stated.

"No, no, no. This is my gift. And you *can* purchase as much as you'd like, but you'll have to come up to the vineyards to do that. We brought a limited stash. Besides, you're going to tour the woodshop, right?" Colton patiently waited for an answer as he cleared the rest of the bottles from the table, never taking his eyes off her.

"Of course," Alexis said, as her pulse began to race. She grabbed a cocktail napkin and blotted her neck, hoping that Colton hadn't noticed that she was now perspiring.

"Great! You have my card. Just call or text me with a day that works for you." Colton examined Alexis's face. "Hey, be sure to wear jeans. It's a bit dusty around the shop. And boots. We'll explore the vineyards. Sound good?"

"Yeah, that sounds like fun," she said, blotting her neck again and feeling self-conscious. It had been a long time since anyone had made her so nervous. "I need some things for the mountain house and all," she said, fidgeting. "You know, the mantel? Maybe some Adirondack chairs."

"Yeah, sure. Whatever you want," he answered and turned to the assistant at the table. "Sam, can you hand me the Pinot Noir behind the table? There should only be one bottle there." Sam handed Colton the reserved bottle. "Here," Colton offered it to Alexis. "This is for you." Alexis took the bottle and both held it and lingered for a moment. Colton smiled. "I look forward to seeing you soon."

"Thanks," Alexis said blushing slightly. "I look forward to it, too. I mean seeing the woodshop and, the vineyards and all," she said feeling even more awkward. "Anyway, thank you," she said and extended her hand. Colton smiled as he accepted the hand shake. Alexis turned and joined her friends.

"Seeing the woodshop and vineyards and all?" Alexis whispered to herself.

"Are you sweating?" Jill asked as Alexis approached them.

"Is it noticeable?" Alexis blotted her neck again.

"Not if we were sitting at the beach!" Jill answered and laughed.

"Jill, it's not funny. I made a darned fool out of myself. I was so nervous! I don't know why," Alexis confessed.

"Well, it's been a while! See? This is why you need to get out more!" Faye stated confidently. "Now aren't you glad you joined us?"

"Did I have a choice?" Alexis smiled and touched Faye's arm. "Yes, I'm glad you forced me to come out. Your mission is accomplished. Now let's get out of here."

The women locked arms, exited the building, piled into a taxi and headed home.

Chapter Four

"Knock! Knock!" Jill peeked her head around the front door of Alexis's home. "Hey!" she exclaimed as she stepped inside. "No pajamas today?"

Alexis stood behind her Christmas tree, positioning an ornament and poked her head out. "Nope. No PJ's!" She stepped out from behind the tree. "You're just in time to help me decorate! Grab a box of ornaments and get busy!"

"Everything looks so pretty! Is this the last tree?" Jill closed the front door and removed her coat, placing it on the living room sofa.

"Yeah. Except the one at the mountain home," Alexis stated.

"When are we going up there?" Jill sorted through several boxes of ornaments laying on the floor and chose one stuffed with glittery red bulbs.

"Well, I have a book event on Saturday in Tranquility and hoped you and Faye would like to join me," Alexis stated. "Pamela's out of town, so it will just be the three of us."

"I thought you were supposed to meet Mr. Hunky at the vineyards," Jill gave Alexis a grin.

"Mr. Hunky can wait." Alexis placed a bulb on the tree. "Except I really do need to order a mantle for the fireplace."

"So? Who says that you can't do both? Go visit his workshop, silly girl! What's the big deal?" Jill asked, eyeing the tree for an empty spot.

"No big deal," Alexis answered.

"Well? Then let's go! We can pick up the tree, you can get a mantle and we can taste some wines!" Jill raised her eyebrows in anticipation of an answer.

"Event first and then we'll see," Alexis said as she peeked around the tree.

"Oh, I see. Now that we're back at the house, she's getting all comfortable again," Jill said as she shook her head and secured her ornament.

"I'm in the room! I can hear you!" Alexis teased. "And I am *not* getting comfortable! I just have a lot to take care of. The mountain house, my novel, my Gran."

"Uh huh." Jill stepped back from the tree, folded her arms and stared at her.

"What?" Alexis smiled and grinned.

"What do you mean 'what?' You have an opportunity, my dear girl. It's time to take it. Start living that beautiful life of yours!"

Alexis sighed, placed her box of ornaments on a table and sat down on the couch. "Jill," she said, paused and sighed.

"What? Are you ill? Is something wrong?"

"No," Alexis chuckled. "I'm fine. It's just that, well, it's been a long time since I've trusted anyone. I know it's not a big deal. I mean, I just met the guy, but he makes me nervous! The whole situation makes me nervous."

"That's it? Geez, I thought it was something serious!" Jill smirked.

"It is serious! I'm gun shy. It's been so easy to hide away from the world," Alexis said as she looked at the tree with a sad expression.

"I know, hon. But, it's time to get back out there. You're not alone. You have us girls and your Gran." Jill stopped and became serious. "So, this guy Colton. He seems to have some kind of an effect on you."

"You could say that. I've only met him twice," Alexis brushed it off. "It's ridiculous."

"Yeah, but there's something about him. I don't think I've ever seen you like this." Jill watched Alexis carefully.

"He makes me uncomfortable. In a good way, you know? I'm sure it doesn't mean anything," Alexis walked to the tree and resumed decorating.

"I think it means a lot. Here you are, at Creekside, you run into him and then again at the wine tasting? And how strange is it that he owns a vineyard right by your mountain home! I'd say that fate had a pretty big part to play in that, don't you?"

"I said that very thing to him," Alexis replied.

"Oh really? And what did he say?" Jill stopped to listen.

"He said we'd have to explore it further," Alexis grinned.

"Well, that sounds like a lot more than just someone sharing wines and Adirondack chairs!" Jill paused. "Alexis, you need to go with this and stop thinking so much. Look at your Gran, flirting and having fun! We can learn from her. Speaking of, how *is* your Gran?" Jill asked.

"Doing great. She had a 'date' with Mr. Winters," Alexis grinned.

"No! Really? That's awesome!" Jill laughed. "Your Gran is so cool." She paused. "Hey, wait. If she and Mr. Winters get married, that would mean that he would be your Step Grand Dad, and Colton would be your . . . cousin? Is that how that works?"

"Oh, stop! And, no, I'm pretty sure that Colton would not qualify as my cousin," Alexis giggled. "But, they do seem to enjoy one another's company. They dine together, watch television. She seems more coherent. I think he's good for her, you know, having a friend and someone her age to talk to," Alexis said.

"That's adorable. Your Gran is a feisty one! I hope I'm as cool at her age." Jill responded. "So, has Michael shared any important information lately?" she asked as the two continued to load up the tree with glitter and shine.

"It's hard to tell. Gran goes in and out of being coherent. During my last visit, Michael had an odd message for me." She wrinkled her forehead.

"Do tell," Jill paused to listen.

"Well, he said that 'mistletoe' will be my sign, like a fork in the road or something. Oh, and I'm not supposed to make fun of the mistletoe." Alexis watched as Jill's expression turned to confusion. "I told you! I can't take any of it seriously. She gives me these cryptic messages and I have no idea what they mean!" she continued.

"Mistletoe, huh? Well, then! We'll have to keep our eye out for mistletoe, whatever that means," Jill responded as the two laughed.

"Come on, let's finish this up and I'll cook you a nice dinner," Alexis offered.

"Deal," Jill answered.

The sun quickly sank below the horizon as the Christmas tree dazzled in the now darkened room. The friends continued to chat and laugh as they headed to the kitchen.

Chapter Five

"**M**r. Brooks?" Alexis opened the front door of her mountain home. Before her stood a stocky, middle aged man, with thinning brown hair, dressed in a deep blue work shirt and worn jeans. His protruding belly pulled at the bottom button of his shirt and his warm smile revealed a gap in his front teeth. He extended his hand.

"Yes, Ma'am! Andrew Brooks. You can call me Andy. Nice to meet you Miss Bradford," he said with a deep southern drawl.

"Oh, please call me Alexis. Come in," she said as she shook his hand and opened the door wide. "As you can see, the basics are in," she said as they made their way through the living room to the open kitchen. "All that is missing is a backsplash. I also need tile work in the bathrooms as I shared with you over the phone." Alexis showed him a display of tiles laid out on the large kitchen island. "Here are the tiles I selected." Alexis picked one up. "This is what I was thinking of using for the half bath and," she picked up a second sample, "this one for the Master. These are from the tile warehouse in town here."

Andy examined the samples. "Shouldn't be a problem, Miss Alexis. I just need to measure. I can pick the tile up tomorrow morning and start the project right away, if you'd like. Did you take a look at the estimate that I sent?"

"Yes, it's fine and tomorrow would be fantastic," she answered. A knock on the door interrupted the conversation. "Excuse me," Alexis said placing the tile down as she made her way to the door.

"Hey! There you are!" she exclaimed as she greeted Jill and Faye now standing on the front porch, suitcases in hand. "Come on in, girls! Glad you could make it!"

"Sorry that we're so late. Traffic heading north was slow," Faye said as she stepped into the foyer. "Oh! The place is beautiful!" she gasped as she looked around the room. An open living area revealed large glass doors that led to a stone patio overlooking acres of woods. The rustic but bright kitchen with a large island opened to a living area with a massive, stone fireplace. Exposed, overhead beams dominated the high ceiling.

"Come, come!" Alexis ordered as she walked through the living room to the glass doors and opened them wide. "Put down your suitcases for a moment! I want to show you something."

"Yes! We want the tour," Jill said as she removed her coat.

Alexis stepped onto the patio. At the center was an outdoor fireplace with views of the Blue Ridge Mountains. "I was thinking of getting Adirondack chairs for this area," she said, pointing to the space, "and maybe one of those big swinging beds."

"Oh I *love* those big beds!" Jill exclaimed. "You could fall asleep out here when you're writing, and take in all of this fresh air!"

"And the bears!" Alexis laughed.

"You have bears out here?" Faye's eyes became large.

"Yeah they have bears out here! Bears and deer and coyotes and raccoons and 'possums and everything else!" Jill explained.

"Alexis, is that true?" Faye asked, still looking shocked. "I mean about the bears!"

"Well, let's just say I wouldn't walk around here at night on my own," Alexis winked at Jill. "Come on inside. I want you to see the living room fireplace. I need a mantel to finish it off." She led the women back inside.

"I'll get busy measuring in the bathrooms now, Miss Alexis," Andy said as he rolled up his measuring tape and headed down the hall.

"This is spectacular! Are these all local materials?" Faye asked.

"Yeah, the beams, too. They actually came off the property." Alexis pointed at the thick wood that spanned the entire ceiling.

"Alexis, this is a perfect getaway! I'm so excited about the weekend!" Faye exclaimed.

"Now I hate to rush you, but we need to leave for my book signing shortly! We'll finish the tour when we get back," Alexis stated.

"Oh, right! We need to go get all prettied up!" Faye said.

Alexis placed her hands on her hips and grinned at them. "You don't have to get all gussied up. This is just a casual, small town event." She walked to the staircase. "I have two bathrooms and two guest rooms upstairs. You have fresh sheets and towels. I think you'll be very comfortable." Alexis picked up Faye's suitcase and walked it to the top of the open staircase that overlooked the living room.

"Oh, and valet service is included! Nice." Faye nodded to Jill who picked up her own case and followed the women.

"I'll meet you both downstairs. You can fight over which bedroom you want," Alexis teased as she put down Faye's suitcase and walked back down the staircase. "Make it snappy!"

Jill ran down the hallway. "First one gets first pick!" she shouted, laughing and dragging her suitcase.

"Hey!" Faye laughed, as she followed. "Not fair! What happened to my valet?"

Alexis laughed to herself, as she walked to the hallway. "Andy! You about done?"

Andy appeared from the Master bath. "Yep. All set. I'll pick up the tile in the mornin' and I'll be here at around 10am to get to work, providin' your tile is in stock."

"Great! Thank you so much. We'll see you tomorrow," Alexis said and stopped. "Andy, you live in the area, don't you?"

"Yes ma'am, I do," he answered as they walked to the front door.

"Do you know anything about the wood mill nearby? The one that is on the Winters Vineyards?" Alexis asked.

"Oh yes ma'am. Everyone knows about the Winters Wood Mill. It's been there for as long as I can remember. Been run by generations.

I use them for my custom pieces, like the mantel I heard you mention. You'll get anything you want there, Miss Alexis. Quality wood and real perty finishes. Yep, you'll be *real* happy with the Winters Wood Mill."

"Thanks, Andy. I may need you to install a mantel soon," Alexis shared.

"Oh sure, Miss Alexis. That's no problem. I'll get one of my workers out here to help and we can fix up anything you'd like," he responded.

Alexis opened the door, thanked and bid him farewell before heading to her Master Bedroom where a little black dress and leather jacket were carefully placed on the bed. She walked into her bathroom and looked in the mirror before pulling a makeup kit out of a cabinet drawer. She leaned close to the mirror and examined her face and let out a big sigh before carefully applying a pale pink gloss over her lips. A stroke of blush on her cheeks and diamond studded earrings were the final touch. It felt good to get dressed up.

Alexis slipped into her dress, stepped before a full-length mirror, turned sideways and ran her hands over her slender stomach and hips. "Alexis Bradford, you're hanging in there, girl!" she said out loud. She opened a drawer, pulled out a brush, and quickly ran it through her hair before slipping into tall, black suede boots. Alexis grabbed her leather jacket and headed to the living room where Jill and Faye were waiting.

"I'm impressed!" Alexis said as she entered the room to find the women relaxing on the sofa. "This is record time for you!"

"Hey, we're not signing books," Faye stated. "But, what is this? You're all dolled up! And look at us!" she said pointing to her jeans.

"You look great! It's a country bookstore and you're right, I'm the one signing books. Jeans and boots are respectable here. People will expect me, however, to show up as the persona of the romance novelist. This is my basic book event uniform," Alexis said as she twirled.

"Well, you look pretty sexy for a writer!" Jill said watching Alexis.

"You'll see for yourselves. The only people that show up at these events are housewives and retirees. If there are more than a dozen people there, I'll be happy," Alexis assured them. "There's a really nice, family run restaurant in town. We can go there afterward if you'd like."

"Sounds good to me," Faye answered.

"Yeah, me too," Jill chimed in. "I could use a good home cooked southern meal. I see a plate of cheese grits in my near future!"

"Now we're talkin'!" Alexis laughed. "Come on, let's get this over with so that we can go get our grits. We don't have far to go. I think you'll love the bookstore. It has an adorable coffee shop and you can hang out while I sign," Alexis said as she grabbed her purse and keys.

The women slipped on their coats and headed out the door and into Alexis's car. As they pulled out of the driveway, Alexis paused to look at the newly constructed stone and wood shingle home that seemed to disappear in the natural setting.

"Alexis, it truly is a beautiful place," Jill said. "It looks like it's been here for years. Thanks so much for having us."

"Are you kidding? I can't tell you how happy I am that you're here! This is what I built it for; sharing with friends. I've dreamed of this place for a long time," Alexis smiled. "My friends are my family now."

"Always," Jill patted her shoulder. "Your parents would be proud of you."

Alexis placed her hand on Jill's. "Thanks." She sighed before putting the car into gear.

The three headed down the narrow, winding road, through thick woods where an occasional clearing revealed rolling hills that stretched for miles. The vast spaces met the base of the mountain range which towered in the distance, covered by a soft mist. Jill and Faye viewed the beautiful landscape, pointing at an occasional deer, as they headed onto a main road and into the small town. They soon arrived at the main street that displayed a handful of storefronts, two restaurants, a pastry and coffee shop and a pub. Alexis continued for another mile until she reached an old farm house that sat back on a large piece of property. Posted in front was a wooden sign "Beau's Book Store" with a drawing of a bull dog and a sign below that stated "Dogs Allowed."

"This is it?" Faye asked.

"Yep, this is it. I told you," Alexis said, "this is no fancy event."

"It's adorable!" Jill exclaimed. "Like something out of one of your novels!"

"I wish!" Alexis laughed. "It's not going to be quite that exciting."

"Well, I agree with Jill. It's adorable. It's an old, converted farmhouse! Jill, we need to explore the grounds. I think there are animals in the back there!" Faye pointed at small buildings and pens filled with pigs and goats located on the grounds. "Now I'm *really* glad that we wore our boots and jeans."

The women stepped out of the car and assisted Alexis in pulling several boxes of books out of the trunk. "Alexis, there are quite a few people standing around," Jill said as she examined the small crowd gathered on the large, wood porch. "It looks like you have quite a few fans."

"Oh, Jill, they aren't here for me. There's a coffee shop inside. It's a small town and I'm sure this is a big hangout for the locals," Alexis replied.

"Are you Alexis Bradford?" a petite blond woman asked as she approached the three women.

"She is," Jill pointed to Alexis. "We're just the help."

"Well, pleased to meet you. I'm Ginny Taylor, the store owner," the woman said as she extended her hand. The people on the porch watched the women and began to chat loudly.

"This is a pretty popular place," Alexis commented.

"Oh no, Ms. Bradford, they're all here to see you," Ginny said.

The crowd excitedly watched as the women walked toward the porch. One by one, guests extended their hands to Alexis as she attempted to shake each.

"Let me get that for you Miss Alexis!" one of the men standing by said as he took her box of books.

"Oh! Well, thank you!" she said looking around at the excited crowd.

"People! Now Ms. Bradford needs to get set up at her table and then y'all can come in and visit. Line up now! Line up!" Ginny shouted. "All Y'all will get your turn!"

Alexis blushed and the friends giggled as Ginny pushed through the crowd that was even thicker inside the store.

"I thought maybe they served great coffee here!" Alexis said under her breath to the girls.

"Alexis! You're a best seller! People know you! I'm not surprised at all!" Faye assured her. "This is a small town and this is a big deal."

"Yeah, Alexis. I think it's great. Come on, we'll help you," Jill said as Ginny showed them to a table set up for the signing. They quickly unpacked the books and stacked them next to a large sign with big bold words, "*An Unexpected Affair*" with Alexis's life sized picture staring at them.

"That's obnoxious," Alexis commented, pointing to the sign. "For the record, my publisher is responsible for this."

Faye and Jill laughed as Ginny busily lined up the dozens of visitors. Alexis barely situated herself behind the table when her first fan pushed her way through.

"Does Melissa get back together with Chad?" a middle-aged woman asked, clutching a Bradford book.

"Now you know I can't tell you . . . what is your name?" Alexis asked.

"Deenie Groves," she answered.

"Deenie, now you don't really want me to spoil it for you, do you?

I *will* tell you that there are a few unexpected surprises for Melissa and a few familiar faces that just might make an appearance!" Alexis teased. The woman giggled loudly and turned to her friend.

"I just love that Melissa! And that Chad, well he is so *bad*! You can't help but love 'em!" Deenie stated. Her friend nodded her head in agreement.

"Hey, we're going to grab a coffee," Jill said, as she leaned over the table between signings. "You've got it covered, right?"

"I'm good. Go have fun and stay out of trouble, and cow pies!" Alexis teased.

"We'll do our best," Faye answered. The two women made their way through the excited crowd to the back of the bookstore, and a small counter. A portly, elderly woman who stood behind it greeted them, and offered hot coffee. Her grey hair was pulled back in a bun, covered with a hair net.

"You gals from the city?" she asked.

"We are. This is Faye and I'm Jill. We're friends of Alexis Bradford," Jill stated proudly. "Your coffee smells great. We'd both love a cup."

"Friends of Miss Bradford? Welcome to Beau's. My name is Eileen and I own this place with my daughter, Ginny. That's Beau there," she said pointing to a fat, old bull dog sleeping near the counter. "You just situate yourselves and let me get you some homemade apple pie to go with that coffee!"

She cut two large slices of the thick pie that oozed sweet apples and placed them on plates before sliding them in a small, electric grill. She quickly filled up two coffee cups in front of the women who parked themselves on stools at the counter. They were soon entrenched in Eileen's stories about the farm house history, the town folklore, and a bit of gossip.

"We're so pleased that you're here, Ms. Bradford," another fan remarked as she slid her book forward. "It's Bobby," she stated. "And

Bobby is me! If you could write somethin' nice, I'd be grateful. My husband didn't believe you'd be comin' to our small mountain town."

"Well, Bobby, you tell your husband that I have my own mountain place here and I love Tranquility. It's the perfect place for me to write." Alexis signed her book. "And let me say that the people here are lovely," she said with a kind smile. Bobby beamed, thanked her and moved on.

The long line slowly moved as Alexis signed each enthusiastic fan's book. Many shared stories with her and spoke of the characters as though real life people. Alexis greeted them all with warmth.

"Can you make this one out to Harry?" the next fan asked.

Alexis looked up to see Colton standing before her, book in hand.

"You can't be serious!" Alexis exclaimed and grinned. "Not another coincidence! You can't tell me that you *really* want me to autograph that book?"

"Of course I do! Besides, like I said, it's for Harry. He's into reading to a certain young lady at Creekside Assisted Living, or so I heard," Colton smiled.

Alexis took the book, shook her head in amusement and signed it. "Assuming you are referring to my Gran, that *'young lady'* probably has this novel memorized. Gran has been captive to my long hours of running storylines past her."

"I don't think she'll mind if Harry reads it to her," he smiled.

"Good point." Alexis grinned, closed the book and handed it to Colton. "So, Colton *is* this another coincidence?"

"No. I admit that it's not. This is a very small town, as you know. A famous person such as yourself making an appearance is a big deal." He held up a flyer with Alexis's picture on it and the event announcement.

"Famous, huh? I'm pretty sure that I don't qualify as famous, but I'll bask in that comment for a few moments," she smiled.

He paused and stepped aside, gesturing for the person behind him to move forward. "Besides," he continued, as he leaned closer, lowering his voice, "I wasn't sure if I'd see you again, so I took it upon myself to *create* another coincidence."

A stout, elderly woman shuffled to the table. "Selma Shelly!" she announced. "To Selma, with love!" she continued, pointing at a blank space where she insisted Alexis sign.

"To . . . my . . . *very dear friend* Selma . . . with love . . . Alexis," Alexis said as she slowly wrote out the words. The woman beamed, clapped her hands, quickly grabbed the book and shuffled away.

Colton leaned in closer. "You didn't tell me that you were famous!"

Alexis grinned. "I wouldn't go that far."

"Well, I'm quite impressed, and I'm glad to see you again and on my turf this time. Now that *you're* here, and *I'm* here in this wee small town with not much to do, why don't we go out for a bite to eat after you finish up?" he whispered.

"I'd like that, but I'm here with Jill and Faye," Alexis answered as she signed the next book. "We were planning on going out to dinner afterward." She handed it back to the fan and looked at Colton. "I wish I could, really. Trust me, I'm looking after your best interests by not having you join us."

"No problem. I didn't expect an invite, but how about tomorrow? You can come out to the vineyards, bring your friends, and I'll take you all on a tour and a tasting," he stood and pushed his hands into his jean pockets. "You can take a look at the wood mill. I'll show you our collection of reclaimed wood for that mantel." Colton stood straight, waiting for her answer.

Alexis hesitated, then smiled. "Yeah. Yeah, I'd like that. I can say with confidence that Jill and Faye will be extremely excited. On their behalf and mine, we accept your invitation. Thank you," she responded.

"Wonderful! How about 4pm? It will be light enough to tour the vineyards and we can all watch the sunset over the property. Then

Dad and I can serve up a nice array of foods from the local farmers. There's a smoked trout dip I think you'll love. It goes really well with several of our white wines." Colton kicked at the floor and smiled. "Sorry. I get carried away with my food and wines. You must think I'm a geek."

"Hardly," she grinned as she greeted the next fan. "I've been accused of being a geek myself, all wrapped up in my writing." Alexis signed the book, paused and looked back at Colton. "I think it's nice. It's good to have passion. Besides, I share your enthusiasm for great food and wine!"

Colton smiled to himself and greeted several of the towns people as Alexis continued signing. Finally, the last book was autographed.

"Wow, I didn't expect that," she said as she stood and stretched her arms to the sky, twisting from side to side.

"Was that the last fan?" Ginny asked as she approached the two.

"It *was* Ginny! That was quite a turnout. I can't thank you enough," Alexis said.

"Well don't thank me! It's you who made it a success. We were so pleased to have Alexis Bradford at our humble book store!"

"It was so heartwarming," Alexis said as she folded her arms and rocked back and forth, stretching her back. "I felt like, well, like I was home."

Colton leaned over and placed his arm around her, giving her shoulder a squeeze. "This *is* your home! Everyone here loves you!"

"They do, Miss Alexis! You can consider us to be your family," Ginny said as she walked to Alexis and squeezed her hand.

Alexis suddenly felt a wave of emotion sweep over her. Her eyes welled up and she quickly wiped a tear that streamed down her face. "I don't know what's come over me!" She laughed, trying to make light of her unexpected emotional response. She quickly attempted to regain her composure. "Thank you. I can't tell you what that means to me." She squeezed Ginny's hand. "I'll pack up everything here."

"Well, you take your time. We'll be serving pie and coffee to our guests so there's no rush!" Ginny responded.

Alexis began to collect several books and placed them back into the boxes as Colton assisted.

"Thanks," Alexis said. "About tomorrow, I just want to warn you that my friends are a handful."

"My Dad is a handful. Believe me, he can handle anything. He's a former military colonel," Colton said as he nodded his head and gave her a grin.

"Really? I'll bet he has some stories," Alexis said as she packed the final books.

Colton folded the box top. "He does. Plenty. He's quite the hero."

"Well, I look forward to meeting him," Alexis said as Jill and Faye appeared.

"Hey there! All done?" Faye asked. "Did it go well?"

"Yeah, it was great," Alexis responded. "Did you have fun?"

"We did! We got into a great conversation with Eileen back in the coffee shop. She's Ginny's Mom. Did you know she makes all of the pies here?"

"And she promised us a tour of the grounds! They have chickens and sheep and goats and everything here!" Faye exclaimed before she took a deep breath and turned toward Colton. "Oh, sorry. I didn't mean to be rude." She stared at him for a few seconds. "Hey, aren't you the man at the wine tasting in Atlanta?"

"First of all, if you are planning on hanging with pigs and chickens, I'm glad that you wore your jeans and especially your boots," Alexis stated. "And, yes, Colton's family owns the Winters Vineyards nearby. They made the wine that we enjoyed the other day. You remember?" Alexis gave Jill a wink.

"Oh, right. So, you have a vineyard nearby?" Jill asked, acting casual.

"Yes," Alexis interrupted. "He's invited us all for a tour and tasting tomorrow."

"Really?" Faye clapped her hands. "That would be lovely!"

"Oh it would! How nice of you!" Jill joined along in the excitement.

"See?" Alexis said, smiling at Colton. "I told you they'd be pleased. We'll see you tomorrow then?"

"What about tonight?" Jill asked. Faye gave her an elbow in the ribs.

"Jill?" Alexis said with a smile and a stern look. "Remember your country dinner? The grits and all that you were looking forward to?"

"We just ate half a pie!" Jill continued, undeterred by Alexis's obvious hint that she wanted to leave.

"I wouldn't want to infringe on your plans," Colton stated.

"Oh, you aren't! We're having a great time here, aren't we Faye?" Jill answered, giving Faye a stare.

"Yes! Yes, we are having a great time here. In fact, Eileen is waiting to give us that tour of the barn and grounds. We'd be so disappointed if we didn't get to go," Faye said.

"Oh really? I didn't know you were so interested in pigs and chickens," Alexis grinned.

"I am!" Faye exclaimed.

"Will you please excuse us for a moment?" Jill smiled, grabbed Alexis by the arm and walked her several feet away. "What are you doing? He's adorable and you're blowing him off to have grits with your girlfriends? You get back there and you invite him for coffee and pie. We can go to dinner afterward. Faye and I are going to spend time with the pigs while you bond! That's an order!" Jill stated.

"I'll see him tomorrow, Jill. This was our girls weekend," Alexis argued.

"That's ridiculous and you know it. It's time to engage in the real world, Alexis. That includes having a coffee and a laugh with that lovely man over there. Now go!" Jill said as she gave Alexis a slight push.

"Well," Alexis said with a forced smile. "It seems that my friends had their hearts set on that tour of the farm." Faye and Jill nodded their heads. "And I wouldn't want to disappoint them. Perhaps we could have that pie and coffee after all."

"Great!" Colton beamed. "Here. Let me help you take these books to your car," he said as he quickly picked up a box.

"That'd be great," Alexis answered. "Thank you."

"We'd best be getting back to Eileen about that tour of the farm," Jill said and winked.

"Yeah, I can't wait to see those pigs!" Faye chimed in as Jill grabbed her arm. "We'll see you shortly!" she shouted as she was whisked away.

Alexis and Colton stood, smiling at one another. Alexis grinned. "Not so subtle, huh?"

Colton laughed. "They obviously care about you." The two walked out the door and to the parking area. "So, how long have you been living in Peaceful Cove?" he asked.

"The house was recently finished. But, I've been coming to this area since I was a kid." Alexis opened her car trunk and they placed the books inside. She paused, closed the trunk and looked at the mountains that were now illuminated by the bluish white light of the moon. "My Dad used to take me fishing on the river. I was an only child." Alexis said as they started to walk back to the bookstore.

"Same here. An only child, I mean. My Dad and I would go fishing, on Tranquility too. Still do." Colton looked at Alexis for a moment. "Hey, you should come join us some time!"

"Oh, I don't know. It's been a long time since I've fished. Not sure I have the wrist action down," she smiled.

"Sure you do. You never forget that!" Colton said as they reached the porch and he held the door open for her. "Well, the invitation is always open." The two made their way to the coffee shop and situated themselves at a small table.

"Two hot coffees?" Eileen shouted from behind the counter.

"And two pieces of that great apple pie, Eileen," Colton smiled. He looked at Alexis. "Are you in?"

"That's perfect," she smiled.

"So, do you still fish with your Dad?" Colton asked.

"Dad passed away three years ago, shortly after my Mom," she answered.

"Wow, I'm so sorry to hear that." Colton reached across the table and placed his hand over hers. "It's difficult, especially over the holidays. I understand why you're so close to your friends."

"Yeah, they're pretty much all I have besides my Gran," she shared.

"I know how that feels. We lost my Mom a few years ago." He looked off into the distance and smiled. "She was somethin'. Kept us in line. We lost my grandmother before Mom, so she was stuck with a house full of boys. Then she got sick. It was a challenging time for us, especially my Dad. He's a tough guy, but it was hard on him." He paused and looked at Alexis. "They were close. She was his soul mate."

"I understand," Alexis now placed her hand over his.

"We all took care of her. It was difficult. So, after she died, Dad and I decided to travel for a while. Gus held down the fort along with my cousin, Jackson. That's when we visited vineyards overseas and entrenched ourselves in expanding our knowledge in the art of wine making. Life was fun again."

Eileen placed two cups of steaming coffee on the table. "I'll be right back with that pie," she smiled. "And then I need to check on those city girls and make sure they haven't fallen into the pig pen!"

"Thanks, Eileen." Alexis laughed and turned back to Colton. "That explains your wine expertise."

"It's Gus and my Dad who have spent their lives perfecting the wines. I can't take much credit for that." He paused. "I'm really glad that you're coming out to the vineyards tomorrow."

Eileen placed two pieces of steaming apple pie in front of them and pulled two forks and napkins from her apron, placing them on the table. "On the house!" she said. "We haven't had anyone famous here, well, ever!"

"Eileen, thank you. It's really not necessary," Alexis blushed.

"It's my pleasure. Now I need to go find those two friends of yours!" she shook her head and grinned.

Colton grabbed his fork and lifted it. "To friends and family!" he said, waiting for her to toast.

Alexis lifted her fork, clinking it into his. "To friends and family!" They smiled and took a bite of pie. "Now I see why this place is so popular!"

The two ate in silence for a few minutes. "So what's in store for Christmas?" Colton asked.

"Dinner with Gran at Creekside, time with friends. How about yourself? I'll bet you have a big celebration at the vineyards," Alexis said.

"Not so big. We pretty much shut it down for the holidays. It's slow this time of year. We take time to regroup. Of course, we'll be spending time with Gus." Colton took another bite and sipped his coffee. "My guess is that ol' Harry and Fifi will be spending time together," he laughed.

"Yep, Fifi is smitten with Harry," Alexis took a bite of pie and smiled. "It's nice. I guess it goes to show that you never know what life may bring, no matter how late it arrives."

"Yeah', you just never know." He looked at Alexis and winked.

"Hey!" Jill and Faye yelled as they ran to the table, out of breath. "I see you got into the pie!" Jill pointed and smiled.

"It's pretty amazing," Alexis responded. "And look at you two," she said pointing to their muddy boots.

"I know!" Faye exclaimed, still out of breath. "We were chasing a little pig that got out of the pen. Woo! Don't be fooled. They can run!" She and Jill laughed loudly still breathing heavy.

"You two never cease to amaze me," Alexis shook her head. "Are you about ready to head out?"

"Sounds good," Jill said. "I think we'll go wash up."

Alexis nodded and stood. "I guess this is good bye again," she said extending her hand to Colton.

Colton took her hand in his and kissed it. "Ms. Bradford, it was an honor to meet such a talented and beautiful celebrity. I'm sure that Harry will love the book," he said with a grin.

Alexis smiled. "Well, thank you for coming."

"Ladies?" Colton saluted the girls who were a few steps away watching. "It was a pleasure!" He turned toward Eileen who was taking her place behind the counter to serve other patrons. "Thank you, Eileen. Everything was outstanding as always!"

Eileen waved and showed a big, toothy smile.

Colton headed out, stopping to greet several locals along the way.

Jill and Fay were silent as they stared, watching his every move as he shook hands and chatted with folks.

"Well?" Alexis said. "Are you going to go wash up?" The two continued to stare in silence. "Girls! Really?!"

Jill turned to Alexis, her mouth open. "You can't be serious. Are you blind? He's gorgeous!" She turned back to watch Colton, who was still laughing and chatting.

Alexis examined him carefully. "Hmm. Yeah, he's a nice-looking guy."

"*Nice* looking? *Nice*? He's much better than Chad!" Faye chimed in.

"That's because Chad is a fictional character, Faye. And that picture of him on the cover of my book is a model, not Chad. Chad isn't real. You're starting to sound like my readers," Alexis teased. "Go clean up and let's get out of here." Alexis grabbed the plates on the table and walked them to the counter before making her way to the entrance where Ginny stood.

"Alexis, this was a great success! Thank you so much for visiting my humble little book store!" Ginny said as she touched Alexis's shoulder.

"It was an honor!" Alexis gave her a long hug.

"Oh! Well, dear, the pleasure was ours. I hope that you will come back soon!"

"Of course. I would be happy to," Alexis answered.

Faye and Jill appeared and the three women made their way out of the bookstore and to their car. The bright, full moon casted shadows on the ground. Alexis turned to look at the old farmhouse. The interior lights glowed softly, and gas lanterns revealed a wooden porch swing and several rocking chairs. The place was still buzzing with locals drinking coffee and visiting.

Jill put her arm around Alexis. "It's nice here, isn't it? Has real charm," she said as she squeezed her shoulder.

"It does," Alexis smiled. "It just feels good."

The two women stared at the pleasant scene for a moment.

Alexis nodded. "Come on. Let's go get those grits!"

The women piled in the car and slowly pulled out of the drive, making their way to the town square and their southern, home cooked meal.

Chapter Six

"Ready ladies?" Alexis asked as she entered the living room. "Absolutely!" Jill declared.

"Alexis, it's so relaxing here," Faye said as she put on her coat. "This is just so great, isn't it?"

Alexis laughed. "What's so great?"

"The book signing, Colton showing up to see you, going to this wine tasting. And I keep thinking about those great stories Eileen was sharing about the farmhouse, and the local people."

"Alexis, this town is really sweet," Jill commented.

"Aren't so 'bumpkin' as you thought they'd be?" Alexis raised her eyebrow.

"Well, yeah. Eileen and Ginny were nice ladies. Did you know that Eileen makes all of the pies for the bookstore and local restaurants too?"

"After eating a piece, I can see why!"

"So, are you nervous?" Jill asked.

"You mean about Colton?" Alexis grinned. "A little."

"I was wondering, you know," Jill stuttered. "I was wondering if maybe, you know," Jill smiled wide.

"No, I don't know," Alexis stared at her.

"Well, if maybe you felt a real connection with him. Maybe a little love connection? Maybe?" Jill teased.

"Get in Jill," Alexis fought off a smile as they made their way to her car.

"Is that a 'yes?'" Jill asked as she slid into the passenger seat.

"I plead the fifth!" Alexis responded. She pulled on her seat belt and put the car into drive.

The three quickly departed and made the fifteen-minute drive past apple orchards, pristine farm land, mountain shacks, and roadside markets. The narrow, dirt road snaked past trees and creeks until it opened to acres of grass laden fields and rolling hills. The car kicked up dust on the rocky, dirt drive as they arrived at their destination, a European style building sitting alone in the middle of acres of land.

"How incredibly charming," Faye said as the women sat and stared.

"It is," Alexis agreed with surprise. "I didn't expect this." They sat in the car for a few moments, viewing the surroundings.

"What did you expect?" Jill asked.

"I don't know. Not anything quite this sophisticated," she responded.

They sat in silence for a few moments. "I guess we should get out, huh?" Faye asked.

"Yeah, let's do it," Jill agreed. The three exited the car and made their way to the entrance. "It's so peaceful," Jill commented as she stopped and stared at the rows of vines that stretched for acres, neatly tended to and waiting for Spring to arrive.

They pulled open two heavy, carved, wooden doors and stepped into an open room with two-story windows that overlooked the property. A massive stone fireplace dominated and an oak tasting bar spanned the length of one wall. On the opposite side, several glass doors lead to a large, screened in porch. Several tables and chairs filled each room.

"Well, hello there!" Colton appeared from a doorway behind the bar. "I saw a car pull up from my office window and was hoping it was you! Welcome, ladies!" He walked into the room and hugged each woman, lingering a bit longer with Alexis.

"Your place is beautiful," Jill commented.

"It's been a work in progress," Colton smiled. "It was once a small, rustic building that included Great Grand Dad's living quarters. When he met my Great Grandmother, he decided that it was time to turn the place into a real home and expand the vineyards. Through the years it's grown and now, it's a full-fledged business as you can see." Colton clapped his hands and then rubbed them together. "So! If y'all are ready, I have a golf cart parked out back and we can get started on our tour!"

"That sounds great," Alexis responded, showing excitement which brought a smile to Colton's face.

"Well then, step this way ladies," Colton said as he led them to a door and down a staircase to the level below. The three friends followed him to the golf cart where Alexis took the seat next to him.

"This is going to be so much fun!" Faye exclaimed.

"Now, hang on there, Faye," Colton ordered. "We may hit a few pot holes along the way. Ladies, are you ready?"

"Ready!" Jill announced as Faye and Alexis nodded their heads.

Colton put the cart into gear and quietly rolled down a small hill and onto a path between the rows of vines. The cart hit a small pothole and popped up sending Faye and Jill off their seats, prompting loud laughter.

"This is like an amusement ride!" Faye shouted as she held tightly to a side handle.

"Better!" Jill added. "They serve wine after this ride!"

Colton sped down the pathway, eventually slowed down and stopped.

"There," he pointed. "That's where we'll be harvesting our next crop. All of this land as far as you can see is part of the vineyards." They were now situated on the top of a hill that revealed acres of cleared land before them. The four sat silently staring as the December sky turned a bright orange and fuchsia.

Colton stepped out of the cart and walked to Alexis's side, extending his hand. "Come with me," he said. She looked him in the eyes and placed her hand in his. "Ladies, let's go for a little walk. I want to show you something." Faye and Jill hopped off the back seat and followed the couple.

"Over here," Colton pointed. "The Pinot Noir. Our award-winning wine. This is where we harvest those grapes." He walked to several vines and stopped. "The sun and soil are perfect here." He gently pulled on one of the now barren stems and examined it. "Amazing, isn't it? These empty vines will produce beautiful, sweet grapes and eventually end up in a bottle on a dinner table or maybe even a wedding." He stared at the vines with affection.

"They're like old friends," Alexis smiled. Colton looked at her with curiosity. "I mean the vines. You count on them. You nurture them and they give so much back in return. But, it's not about that."

Colton stared at her with a look of surprise. "That was quite poetic," he smiled. "And insightful."

"She's a very good writer," Jill reminded him.

"I see the look in your eyes. You have real passion for this. These aren't just vines," she said as she looked at the rows before her.

"You're right about that," Colton agreed. "It's my legacy. It's our way of life. In the Spring, this property will look like a completely different place. It will be bustling and full, and green. And another season of our lives begins." He looked over the land as though imagining the scene described. "Dad, Jackson and I will be here, constantly checking on the grapes, waiting for that perfect moment."

"Who's Jackson?" Jill asked.

"My cousin," Colton answered. "He works here on the grounds. A sort of vintner in training. You'll get to meet him shortly." He turned toward the women. "Come. Let's tour the rest of the property and enjoy this sunset. We have food and wine waiting for us." The clouds were now morphing and taking on darker pinks, blues and purple.

The friends hopped in the golf cart and made their way around the property, up and down the pathways. Colton purposely hit an occasional pot hole, prompting screams from Faye and Jill. Darkness quickly set in as they made their way back to the winery and up the stairs to the main tasting room. There, laid out on a long table, were plates of food, cheeses, and several wine glasses.

"It looks like Jackson set everything up for us!" Colton stated.

"And perhaps your good ol' Dad helped just a bit." A tall, large framed, grey haired man appeared from behind the bar, carrying several bottles of wine.

"Dad! Thanks," Colton smiled as he took the bottles and placed them on the table. "I'd like you to meet my friends. This is Alexis, Faye, and Jill."

"A pleasure to meet you, young ladies. Did you enjoy a tour of the grounds and our breathtaking sunset?" he asked.

"It was beautiful," Alexis replied. "It must be wonderful living here, in the middle of all this beauty."

"It is indeed," he answered. "Let me introduce myself. I'm obviously Colton's Dad. My name is Carl." He extended his hand to each of the women. "Welcome to Winters Vineyards."

"Thank you so much for having us," Alexis said.

"Take a seat," he ordered as he pulled out a chair. "Let's get to some wine tasting and eats!"

The group took their place at the table, chatting and tasting as Colton poured wines all around. Carl and Colton took turns explaining the origins of each along with stories of their travels.

"So, you've spent time in Europe!" Jill confirmed.

"Yes, we collaborate with several vineyards, primarily in France. We credit some of our award-winning wines to the training and support we've received from them. We also carry their wines," he explained as he leaned forward and grabbed a bottle. "Here. This is one. An outstanding French family vineyard." He stood and poured the wine into each glass as he walked around the table.

"France isn't such a bad place to *have* to visit!" Alexis smiled.

"Colton had an opportunity to live there," Carl said as he gave Colton a grin.

"Well, I'm not as fond of France as my Dad," Colton quickly added. "It's nice to visit, but I'm perfectly happy here in Tranquility."

"Oh really?" Alexis said with a raised eyebrow. "You wouldn't have to twist my arm to move to France."

Colton took a sip of his wine. "So, ladies, what do you think of this one?" he asked, suddenly changing the subject. "This is a new blend." He stuck his nose in the glass and took a long sniff.

"It's very good!" Faye commented.

"Yes, excellent," Jill agreed.

Alexis took a sniff as she watched Colton. She sensed that the discussion about France was over. "Mr. Winters," she began.

"Oh, please, call me Carl," he insisted.

"Okay. Carl, besides your passion for woodworking and wines, Colton tells me that you served our country," she continued.

"Dad was one of the first responders in the Gulf war. He's a retired Lieutenant Colonel," Colton said with pride.

"That's impressive!" Faye exclaimed. "How does a Lieutenant Colonel end up making wines?"

"Generations," Alexis answered.

"It's true. My Great Grand Dad tinkered with wine. He was the original wood worker. He owned this property and started growing grapes. It's in our blood and our soil," Colton said as he paused and looked at Alexis. "That reminds me. Would you like to visit the wood mill? We can take a quick tour of the place and talk about that mantel piece."

"Yes! Go and explore the wood mill. I'll keep Faye and Jill busy here. We have plenty more wines to try," Carl said as he raised his glass.

"Well, I certainly would love to hear some stories about your service," Jill said.

"I would too!" Faye chimed in.

"I have plenty to share!" Carl said, noticeably pleased to have such engaged company. He looked up. "Uh oh, just when I thought I had them all to myself!"

"Hello ladies!" A lanky, good looking man entered wearing loose jeans, a plaid shirt and baseball cap. "I'm Jackson. Pleased to meet you," he said as he went around the table and shook hands.

"Jackson here is my cousin," Colton boldly stated. "Take a seat Jackson, and pour some wines."

Jill was mesmerized. "Yes! Please! Take a seat, Jackson," she said as she pulled out the chair next to her and patted the seat. Jackson smiled and swaggered over, pulled the chair out further and flipped it around to sit on it backward. He sat, legs astride and put both arms over the back of the chair.

"Don't mind if I do!" he smiled, watching Jill who now acted shy. "You gals from the city?" he asked.

Colton stood and pulled Alexis's chair out. He leaned down and whispered in her ear, "It looks like your friends are in good hands." She giggled as they made their way out of the room and back to the golf cart.

Colton lifted a blanket off the seat and placed it around Alexis's shoulders. "It's getting chilly out here," he said as he made his way to the driver's seat and put the cart into gear. "Hang on!" They sped down a pathway to the end of the property where a large, two story, log building stood. Gas lit lanterns located on each side of the double entry doors cast a soft light on the ground. Inside, metal industrial hanging lamps created a glow that lit up the interior.

"Is this the original building?" Alexis asked as she hopped out of the cart.

"It is. We've pretty much just maintained it. Come with me," he said, extending his hand and helping her navigate the pathway. "Welcome to over 150 years of work, sweat and love," he said as he helped Alexis onto the porch, pushing the front door wide open. "Enter, my lady!"

"Wow!" she gasped as she took in the magnitude of the space. "Colton, this is beautiful." She gazed around the well-organized room with its high beamed ceiling. Several long, heavy, wood working tables were lined up. The remainder of the space housed large saws, heavy machinery, storage cabinets, and tools that were careful stored on the walls. The cold stone floor revealed years of wear.

"So, this is where generations made beautiful things," Alexis said as she slowly walked around the room, running her hand over several pieces of partially finished furniture.

"And still do," Colton said as he walked to a door and opened it. "Here. This is what I want to show you." He motioned her to join him.

Alexis gently ran her hand over the tables and equipment as she made her way to the door, feeling the energy of years of craftsmanship. She entered the adjoining room, filled with finished pieces of finely crafted furniture that included coffee tables, patio furniture, mantels, buffets, and smaller pieces such as polished, wood bowls. Each unique, showed the soft lines of transformed trees.

"I'm home!" Alexis laughed. "How could I not know about this place?"

"Well we *are* tucked away at the back of the property here. Great Grand Dad started out making custom pieces for locals and we expanded to contractors and builders. We haven't promoted much to the public although they are always welcome. I guess you could say that we're a local secret," Colton said as he ran his hand over the arm of an Adirondack chair. "My guess is that you've spent most of your time in the city?" He looked at her, raised his eyebrows and smiled.

"Other than my time here as a kid, that would be correct. I'm not exactly an official member of the Tranquility community, but now that the house is complete, I'll be spending more time here. I do love it," she said, giving Colton a sheepish grin.

"That's great news!" Colton exclaimed looking a little embarrassed at his enthusiastic response. "Sorry," he grinned. "It's just that I think you're a breath of fresh air."

Alexis looked at him and smiled. "Thanks."

"So, if you'd like, you can come back here and we can spend more time on this, come up with some ideas and sketches. I'll show you where we store our reclaimed wood, and maybe something will catch your eye. We can custom make pretty much anything. Whatever you want, Alexis." Colton looked directly at her. His face softened. The two looked at one another in an awkward silence.

"I'd like that," Alexis said, then giggled. "I mean, you know, coming up with ideas and sketching and all that."

"Yeah, of course. You just let me know." He smiled and walked to the door. "Well . . . let's get back to the tasting room," Colton said and paused. "I'm glad I got to show you the shop."

"You have a lot to be proud of Colton," Alexis responded.

Colton suddenly stepped forward and gave her a long, lingering kiss.

"Sorry, Alexis," he said as he looked deep into her eyes. "I couldn't help myself. There's something very special about you." He paused. "I know that we hardly know one another, but I'm drawn to you."

She smiled. "I'm really glad that we met."

"Fate, right?" he grinned.

"Yeah. Fate," Alexis agreed.

"You caught my eye that very first day at Creekside." He grabbed her hand. "Come on. Let's head back to the tasting room. I have something special to share with you. Ready?"

"Absolutely," she responded.

Colton shut off the lights and closed the door behind them, as they made their way back through the woodshop and to the golf cart. Alexis pulled the blanket around her shoulders as they silently sped back through the property. The bright moon lit up the surrounding trees casting shadows on the vineyards as they drove between the straight rows.

Alexis took in a deep breath and looked up at the dazzling stars. "The sky is incredibly clear in Tranquility!"

"No light pollution. Pure nature!" Colton responded. "God's country!" He took in a deep breath and looked up at the sky as they pulled up to the main building and parked.

"Here they are!" Carl Winters announced as the couple entered the room. "Welcome back!" The table was scattered with plates of cheese and food, several bottles of wine and red stained glasses.

"You've been busy!" Colton said as he pulled off his gloves and coat.

"Keeping the gals happy," Carl beamed.

"Carl has been sharing the most amazing stories!" Faye exclaimed. "He's been in some pretty scary situations."

"Oh, not so scary, Faye. It's what a soldier does," Carl nodded his head with a look of pure satisfaction.

"Dad's a hero," Colton said as he stood behind his Father, placing his hands on each shoulder. "I'm proud of him."

Carl reached back and patted Colton's hand. "I'm proud of my boy here. He's done a great job of running this place and taking on a lot of responsibility. Kept us going, even during our toughest times."

Colton gave an understanding look then squeezed his Dad's shoulders in a fun-loving manner to lighten the mood. "So!" Colton exclaimed as he stood straight. "Now for the pride and joy of Winters Vineyards!" He reached into a wooden case and pulled out a bottle with a unique label. "Our award winner and tribute to my Great Great Grandfather, 'Wooden Mistletoe.'" He lifted the bottle for all to see.

"Wooden Mistletoe?" Alexis stared at the bottle.

"Yeah," Colton laughed. He looked at his father who smiled. "It's sort of a corny story. Great Great Grandad was a humble guy."

"That's code for 'short on cash,'" Carl teased, prompting everyone to laugh.

"Exactly. Well, it was Christmas time and he wanted to present my Great Great Gran with something special. He wanted to propose and he couldn't afford a ring, so he did what he does best. He took a piece of wood and carved it into, well, mistletoe."

"Thus, the Wooden Mistletoe," Alexis said slowly as she made eye contact with Jill.

"Yep, Wooden Mistletoe. He hung it over her head and proposed to her. Each generation proposes under that mistletoe." He pointed to a spot over the entrance door where a hand carved mistletoe hung. "And there it is! It's corny, but it's tradition."

Alexis and Jill stared at the object. Alexis's mouth dropped open and her eyes widened. "No, it's not corny." She paused. "You shouldn't make fun of mistletoe, you know." Colton gave her a look of confusion. "Never mind. I'll explain later," Alexis said as Jill shook her head in disbelief.

Colton quickly pulled the cork and shared its contents. "I hope you like it!"

Alexis raised her glass. ""To *new* friends! And Wooden Mistletoe!" The six raised their glasses and clinked them as they repeated the cheer. "Mr. Winters and Colton, thank you for inviting us into your lovely establishment. The tour of the grounds and woodworking shop, your generosity, it's been a special evening."

"Well, it's been special for us, too!" Carl said, raising his glass.

"You've been more than generous," Alexis added.

"You aren't leaving, are you? Y'all are welcome to stay longer!" Carl said enthusiastically.

"Ya'll should stay!" Jackson chimed in.

"Unfortunately, I have tile being installed in the morning. But, I plan on visiting the woodshop soon," Alexis announced.

"Name the time," Colton answered with a big smile as he stood. "Jill and Faye, don't you ladies wait too long to come back either!"

"You young gals made an old man very happy tonight. I truly enjoyed your company," Carl shared. "As Colton said, you are always welcome here!" He stood.

Faye, Jill and Alexis took their last sip and stood, putting on their coats as they chatted. They hugged Carl who escorted them to the exit.

Colton followed Alexis who stopped at the door. She looked up at the wooden mistletoe, raised up on her toes and kissed his cheek. "Thank you."

"It's been my pleasure," he said beaming.

The women said their 'thank you's' before walking to their car as Colton escorted them. They waved to Carl and Jackson who stood on the porch watching.

Colton took Alexis's hand in his. "It was great to spend time with you."

Alexis nodded. "Same here."

"I look forward to your call." He smiled as he opened her car door and waited for her to get in. He closed it and waved before walking back to the porch.

"I'm *freaking out*! That can't be a coincidence!" Jill said as soon as Colton was out of ear shot.

"What are you talking about?" Faye asked as she leaned forward from the back seat.

"Oh, just something that Michael said," Alexis said as she waved back at Colton and pulled out of the driveway.

"Michael? Who's Michael?" Faye asked.

"Archangel," Jill responded in a casual manner.

"Archangel Michael? What the heck?" Faye crinkled her brows.

"It's a sign, Alexis!" Jill stared at her as they drove out of the parking lot. "Your fork in the road, remember? Pay attention to the mistletoe! That is insane!"

"A sign for what?" Faye asked.

"It *is* insane, Jill. When I saw that wine label I thought I would pass out. I can't even process it." Alexis paused and looked at Jill. "Do you really think there's a connection?"

"Of course, there's a connection!" Jill looked at Alexis in amazement. "That has to be what the message is referring to! It doesn't get any more obvious!"

"Alright you two. What in the heck are you talking about? Come on! Clue me in!" Faye urged.

Alexis and Jill looked at one another for a moment.

"Hey! Let's sing Christmas carols on the way home!" Alexis exclaimed. "Let's sing Jingle Bells," she suggested as she began to sing loudly. "Jingle bells, jingle bells!"

"Ohhhh! You two!" Faye complained. "I'll get it out of you eventually," she grinned and joined in. "Jingle all the way!"

Jill smiled, winked at Alexis and began to sing.

Chapter Seven

"Young lady, now I told you to go watch television in the lounge!" Mabel said sternly as a small child with long braids entered the room. At age 5, Annabel was smaller than most children and didn't fit in with the other kids at school. She preferred the company of adults and loved to speak of fantastical things, like the invisible friends that often visited her. Annabel grabbed her dress bottom, hand on each side, and swished her skirt back and forth.

"Oh that little Annabel is so sweet. Now Mabel, she's not doing anyone harm. Besides, Annabel and I are good friends, aren't we Annabel?" Gran stated proudly.

"Uh huh," Annabel answered, still swishing her skirt back and forth as she skipped around the room.

"Besides, Annabel knows Michael," Gran added.

"Oh, no, that's not going to happen," Alexis said as she stood in anticipation of escorting the young girl out of the room to protect her from her Grandmother's talk of visions.

"Oh, it's fine, Miss Alexis. I'm afraid it's true. Annabel has a 'gift' of sorts. Doesn't fit in with the kids at school. They make fun of her, her havin' abilities and all," Mabel revealed.

"Abilities?" Alexis stopped and watched as Mabel casually folded towels and stacked them.

"Oh yes, Miss Alexis. She done have the gift from the Lord. Sees angels and all. My Annabel, well, she's just a little girl and she don't know that she shouldn't be tellin' other people about her gift." Mabel smiled at Annabel who giggled. "She don't understand how's people can be so cruel and makin' fun, them not havin' the same gifts."

"Oh," Alexis said, unsure of how to respond. "Nothing wrong with being different. Right Annabel?" Alexis said as she knelt beside the young girl. "So, are you saying that Annabel sees Michael too?" she asked Mabel as she stood up and watched the child smiling and twirling.

"Oh yes! I didn't want to say anything before, as I know you don't especially believe in such things, but it's true. Annabel, well, she sees Michael right here in your Grand Mama's room," Mabel confirmed.

Alexis stared at Mabel, then Annabel, then her Gran who smiled at her and nodded. "I don't know what to say." She sat down in a chair, speechless.

"I know, Miss Alexis. It's hard to believe sometimes, but believin' doesn't require seein' don't you think?" Mabel asked.

"Well," Alexis paused. "I guess not."

"That's what faith is, right Alex? Faith doesn't require any proof!" Gran giggled and went back to a cross word puzzle that she was working on.

"That's right! That is truly right!" Mabel exclaimed. "And sometimes we's thinks we knows something from what we sees, but it 'ain't at all that way." Mabel looked at Alexis and grinned. "Oh I'm not makin' any sense now!"

"No Mabel, you make perfect sense. You really do." Alexis looked at Annabel, whose big smile got even wider. "Annabel, is Michael in the room with us now?" she asked.

Annabel, still swishing the skirt of her dress twirled and threw her arms out, laughing before she stopped. "No," she answered.

"No what?" Mabel asked.

"No Ma'am, Miss Alexis. He's not here right now," she smiled shyly.

"Annabel, why do you think this is such a special place for Michael to hang out?" Alexis asked.

"Oh, he don't stay in just one place!" she exclaimed. "He can be anywhere he wants, all at the same time!" she stated, emphasizing each word.

Mabel continued to fold and stack towels, placing several in Grandma's bathroom, not giving much attention to the conversation.

"Is that so?" Alexis puckered her lips. "That explains a few things."

"Yes Ma'am! He can be here, and there," she said pointing outside, "and at your church, and my church, and in a barn, and at a hospital, and with new babies, and old people, and on the top of a mountain, and,"

"Alright, young lady, we all gets your point," Mabel interrupted her. "Miss Alexis, I'll take Annabel back to the lounge so she can watch some programs and color her books."

"No, it's Okay," Alexis assured Mabel. She got out of her chair, knelt, and took the child's hands in hers. "I believe you, Annabel," she smiled. "I think that you and I are going to be very good friends."

The young girl nodded her head. "Uh huh."

"Good," Alexis smiled and sat back in her chair.

"We'll be on our way, Mrs. B.," Mabel announced then turned to Alexis. "You just let me know what you need. I'll be here for another two hours and then Annabel and I will be goin' home for our supper. Right Annabel?" The young girl nodded strongly again.

"Thank you, Mabel. I think we're fine." Alexis extended her hand. "Nice to see you, Annabel."

Annabel shook her hand and nodded again. "Uh huh."

"Oh, Miss Alexis," Mabel said, motioning her to the door and lowering her voice. "I just wanted to let you know that Mrs. B's been real clear lately. I think Mr. Winters has been good for her."

"Yeah, I've noticed that," Alexis agreed.

"Oh, and about Mr. Winters, I don't know if it's true or if he just likes Mrs. B that much, but he claims to see Michael, too!" Mabel added.

"Really?" Alexis frowned.

"I just wanted to mention that in case he brings it up," she added.

"Thank you Mabel. I appreciate the information," Alexis said as she touched Mabel's hand.

"Bye, Mrs. B! I'll see you tomorrow," Mabel said loudly.

"Bye my angels!" Mrs. B responded and waved.

The two left the room and Alexis sat in amazement. "Huh," she said out loud. "I'm feeling left out."

"Left out of what dear?" her Grandmother asked.

"I seem to be the only one who isn't friends with Michael," she answered.

"Oh!" Gran laughed. "You don't have to worry about that. There are things we don't understand my darling, but you are never left out. You have your own angels. You just need to pay attention. They're with you."

"Oh really? Well, I've yet to see them," Alexis sat back in her chair.

"They don't always appear the way you think they should, Alexis. They aren't always walking around with halos and wings!" she laughed. Her Grandmother paused and looked at Alexis intently. "My sweet little dear, you've allowed your losses to make you question life and to retreat from it."

Alexis looked at her with tears in her eyes. "Have I Gran? It's difficult not to."

"I understand Alexis, but we all experience loss. Yes, it's true that yours has been great in a short period of time. But this is part of being human. These losses can strengthen you and open your eyes to how precious life truly is." She paused. "You get to choose, Alexis."

"Do I Gran?" Alexis stood and grabbed a tissue from her Gran's bedside table. She sniffled and dabbed at her nose.

"You always get to choose. Your angels are with you always, but you choose not to see them. You think that you are alone. You are never alone." Her Gran extended her hand. "Come here my dearest."

Alexis walked to her Gran and took her hand. "When you're ready, the world will open itself up to you. But you can't receive it with those heavy curtains closed. It's time to fling them wide and let the sun shine in. There is nothing to fear."

Suddenly, there was a knock on the door. "Just a moment!" Alexis shouted. She dabbed her eyes and wiped the tears from her face. "Thank you, Gran," she said and kissed her Grandmother's cheek. She stood and straightened her blouse before walking to the door and opening it. There, in his wheelchair, dressed in a formal shirt and wool cardigan was Gus Winters.

"Miss Alexis! What a wonderful pleasure! I am here to escort your Grandmother to the garden and then lunch. I hope that you will be joining us," he said.

"Gran?" Alexis began, "You have a special visitor!"

"Is that my Harry?" she asked.

"Yes, my dearest FiFi! It is Harry!" he said as he wheeled into the room. "Are you ready?"

"I am!" Gran said excitedly. "I'm sorry, Alexis. I forgot to mention that Harry would be picking me up for an outing. You will, of course, join us!"

"Oh, I wouldn't want to butt in," Alexis said.

"But you must!" Mr. Winters insisted.

"Yes! You *must*, Alexis. I am your Grandmother and that is an order!" she said with a stern face.

"Yes, Grandmother," Alexis answered with a sheepish smile. "Let's get you into your chair."

Her Gran smiled proudly at her effective use of power and moved to the edge of the bed where Alexis assisted her into her wheelchair.

"Mr. Winters?" Alexis said, "Please lead the way!"

Alexis pushed her Gran while Mr. Winters wheeled himself out the door and into the hall. The three made their way to the patio. "Gran, are you going to be warm enough?" she asked.

"Oh yes, dear. I just want some fresh air and to look at nature," she replied. Alexis opened the glass French doors that lead to the stone patio, with Mr. Winters following.

The three positioned themselves, overlooking the fields and breathtaking view. Alexis took a seat on a nearby bench. It was totally silent except for an occasional chirp of a bird and breeze that rustled the branches of nearby trees. They sat for several minutes, taking it in.

"You miss your garden, don't you Gran?" Alexis asked.

"Yes, I do," she responded. "I know that I can't dig into the dirt like I used to, but it would be so nice to pot a few herbs and succulents."

"I understand FiFi. I miss my woodshop terribly. Just smelling the fresh cut wood and running my hands over the finished pieces made me happy. It pains my heart not be a part of that," Mr. Winters added.

"Mr. Winters, I visited the woodshop recently. It's beautiful. What you've done there is amazing. In fact, Colton and your son will be creating a mantel and other pieces for me. I can understand how special it is to you."

"Yes, Colton shared that you and your friends visited. They enjoyed their time with you. It's a special place. A part of me is still there," he said looking sad.

"Just a few minutes more, Alexis, and we'll go in and have our lunch," Gran stated.

"That's fine Gran. Whatever you and Mr. Winters want. We can sit out here as long as you'd like," Alexis replied, watching the two friends enjoy the splendor of nature. Alexis observed them, quiet in their thoughts and memories. She sat with her own and the wheels started turning.

Chapter Eight

"Hey there!" Colton exclaimed as Alexis entered the woodshop. "Welcome back! I have everything ready for you." He walked to a large table where drawings were laid out. "I thought we'd look at some of the concepts first and then take a walk back to the barn where we keep the wood collection. I have some beautiful reclaimed pieces that just came in."

"Wonderful," Alexis said, noticeably happy to see Colton. Dressed in jeans, cowboy boots and a sweater, she situated herself on a stool at the table.

Colton pushed one of the drawings toward her and she leaned over it, pushing back a lock of hair. Her skin glowed and her cheeks were rosy from the cold winter air. He couldn't help himself from staring at her.

"I love it," she said, pushing several drawings around.

"Which one?" he asked.

"All of them," she smiled. "These are great. I honestly don't know how to choose."

"I'm glad that you approve," Colton said. "You don't have to pick one right away. In fact, you can take the drawings with you and decide when you're ready. Let's take a walk to the barn. Maybe that will inspire you." He held out his hand which Alexis took as he helped her hop off the stool. She followed him outside and to a barn not far from the woodshop.

"Colton, there's something that I want to talk to you about," she said as they entered the weathered structure. "This might sound a little crazy, but I have to share an idea."

"A little crazy, huh? Well, give me a try," he said with a grin.

She leaned up against the barn wall. "I was just with my Gran and your, well, Harry. We got to talking, and I saw how much they both missed the daily things that they loved before moving to Creekside, like her garden and his woodshop."

"I know. I often think that there must be a way to get Grandad here so that he can get his hands into his work. The shop just isn't built for a wheelchair and the trip back and forth is tiring for him. He really misses it," Colton paused and waited for her reply.

"Well, that's what I was thinking. My Gran misses her garden. It was so important to her. I can see why so many elderly people slowly fade away. They can't do the things that they loved most. It's just not feasible to transport her to my garden, either. It's watching the plants grow and overseeing them every day that she misses."

"I know. We take them out of their most beloved environments and wonder why they become despondent," he agreed.

"Colton, I have an idea. What if we brought the woodshop and garden to our grandparents?" Alexis asked, standing up straight.

"What? I'm not following you."

"Well, think about it. Creekside sits on acres of untouched land, much of which the facility owns. It would be easy to add a garden in the back, accessible to wheelchairs. At the very least, those unable to get their hands into the garden can enjoy the view and the smells. There could be a potting area and classes. There's so much that we could do with that. And your Grandad. We could create a workshop in that empty warehouse attached to the main facility. It could be a place where the residents make simple things, and your Grandad could teach them with supervision. You know, nothing dangerous. But, it would give them back their ability to create and build."

Colton stared at her for a moment. "That's not such a crazy idea." He paused. "I could donate my time to oversee some classes. It'd give me a chance to spend quality time with Gus. We have some machinery and materials that we could donate. Hey! We could have a fundraiser at the winery!" Colton's excitement grew.

"I'll donate proceeds from book signings and get the girls to help with the garden!" Alexis joined in.

"Alexis, I think this would be an incredible contribution to the facility and it would honor our grandparents. Dad will be totally on board with this!" Colton said, getting excited. "Let's get started right away. We can draw up plans and present them to Creekside."

"We can rally the town around this. The Creekside facility is dear to their hearts. Many of the residents have loved ones there," Alexis pointed out.

Colton stepped forward, pulled her in his arms and gave her a long, deep kiss. Alexis froze. Her eyes closed, she took a deep breath and paused. "I guess that means you like the idea?" She opened her eyes and smiled at him, taking another long breath.

"Yeah, you could say that," he grinned. "It's ambitious, but I think that we can handle it." He paused and lifted her chin. "You're a caring person, Alexis. I knew that the first time that I met you. I can't explain it, but there is something incredible between us and, well, I hope you feel the same way."

Alexis smiled and looked at her feet. "I can't believe I'm saying this. I mean, we hardly know each other, but yeah, I do." She paused. "Sometimes you just have to go with your heart, you know?"

Colton smiled and kissed her again. "Yeah, I do know." He grabbed her hand and lead her to the other side of the barn where walls of wood were vertically stacked in rows. "Come on. Choose something special. Take your time and go through every piece. They all tell a story." He walked to one large beam and touched it affectionately. "Like this one that just arrived. This barn was over 200 years old, owned by a local family. It housed animals, took on sun, rain and snow. Held up for generations. It's retired now and ready to serve a new purpose."

Alexis carefully examined it. "It's beautiful." She ran her hand along the weathered piece, it's knots and cracks. She looked at Colton and smiled. "I think it found a home."

"Are you sure? There are a lot more to choose from. You didn't even look at the others. Are you sure you want to go with the first beam you saw?" he asked.

"Yeah, I'm sure. It speaks to me. This is the one. It's perfect. When it's right, you know." They both stood, staring at it. Sun beams shot through slats in the barn walls illuminating dust particles that hung like smoke and swirled. Outside, a Mockingbird sang, and a horse whinnied. Colton took her hand in his, and gave her another long kiss. They stood in silence, taking in the depth of the moment.

Chapter Nine

"Colton, we got the approval!" Alexis burst through the front door of the winery to find it empty. She made her way to the office, then down the stairs to the large tanks of wine where Carl stood, tinkering.

"Hello young lady! It's good to see you. I suppose you're looking for Colton. You'll find him in the dirt cellar," he shared.

"Thanks, Carl," she said, giving him a kiss on the cheek. She quickly walked outside to a small, stone building that housed an underground cave that the Winters family originally used to store their wine during the hot, Georgia summers. It was now a place where Colton tinkered with various wines, tasted and experimented with blends. Alexis noticed a golf cart and SUV parked outside and entered. The small interior had only one large stone table which rested on a dirt floor. It was cold and silent. Small windows carved into the thick, stone walls allowed only a thin ray of light in. Alexis paused to allow her eyes to adjust to the dark room. She made her way to an arched wood door and down a narrow, spiral stone stairwell. At the bottom was a winding, dimly lit catacomb lined with wine racks.

As she made her way along the tunnel, she could hear distant voices. "Colton!" she shouted as she stopped to listen. The voices stopped for a moment. "Colton? Are you down here?" She continued to walk toward what were now whispers until she saw a figure. There stood Colton holding a glass of wine. In front of him, on a small table sat several bottles. Next to him stood a tall, attractive brunette in low heels and a tight, black dress. She too held a glass of wine and had her hand placed on his shoulder. The two suddenly looked up. The beautiful woman smiled and cocked her head to one side, sizing up Alexis.

"Alexis! I didn't hear you come down!" Colton said, looking surprised.

"Well, I was shouting your name," Alexis said as she studied the stranger.

"I'm sorry. Alexis, this is Chantelle," Colton said, "my,"

"Fiancé," Chantelle quickly cut in, with a heavy French accent.

"Chantelle," Colton said with a look of disapproval. He took her hand off his shoulder. "Chantelle is not my fiancé. She is my 'former' fiancé and is one of our suppliers. We carry French wines from her family's vineyards."

"Did I not say 'for-mare'? I am sorry, it eez my English," Chantelle said, her French accent getting heavier, as she flipped her long hair back.

"Your English is perfect, Chantelle," Colton said with a grin. He walked to Alexis and kissed her.

"Not so much since I spend so much time 'een France," she said, flashing a coy smile at Alexis. "Colton, we must make a decision on zees Burgundy wines. I think we must spend more time tasting them, no?"

"No," Colton said. "I'll finish tasting these on my own and then we can discuss which ones Dad and I will order," he stated.

Chantelle pushed her bottom lip out and batted her eyelashes. "Oh, that is so sad. I looked forward to our tasting together." She looked at Alexis, shrugged her shoulders and smiled. Alexis smiled back with effort.

"I think it's time for you to go, Chantelle," Colton said as he picked up an opened bottle, pushed a cork into it and placed it in a box.

"If you say so mon amour," Chantelle responded as she kissed Colton on the cheek, and flipped her hair again. She put her glass of wine down on the table. "I will be back," she said as she picked up a small box of wine, turned and swished out of the cellar, clacking her high heels as she made her way up the stone steps.

"Well, she was charming," Alexis stared at Colton, waiting for an answer.

Colton paused and pushed a box of wine aside. "I'm sorry about that. I should have told you." He took Alexis's hand in his.

"You were engaged?" Alexis sat on the small table stationed against the stone wall trying not to reveal the tremors that now reverberated throughout her entire body. "Care to share the story?" she asked.

Colton took a deep breath and looked at the ground for a moment before proceeding. "It was years ago," he paused. "When we lost my Mom, it was a painful time as I shared with you. It was just Gus, Dad, Jackson and I. She had been our rock." He looked at Alexis with a sorrowful expression. "She had been ill for some time and then, well, there we were without her with only the vineyards and woodshop to keep us busy. As you know, Dad and I traveled to Europe and spent time with vintners, learning from them, and collaborating. It was a great way for us to recover and bond. We entrenched ourselves in our passion. Grand Dad and Jackson held down the fort while we visited places like Italy and France."

"I'm sorry about your mother," Alexis responded. "I'm sure that must have been difficult."

"It took a while to heal, but we pulled together. She would have wanted that." He paused. "I was in France working with an excellent family-owned vineyard when I met Chantelle. It was her family's vineyard. It was a lonely time in my life. I was vulnerable and you can probably guess the rest. We had wine in common and at the time it seemed like a great match." He paused and turned toward Alexis. "But then things can seem magical when you're standing in the middle of the vineyards in France, eating French foods, drinking French wines, and sharing the beauty of the culture."

Alexis stared with a blank expression.

"It felt good to experience excitement . . . to feel alive again." Colton paused, then continued. "Chantelle is a charming woman and

I should have gotten to know her better before we made a commitment. The distance was an issue, and you can't truly know someone through an occasional visit. A lifelong commitment is a serious decision. Eventually, I saw the truth. Chantelle is about Chantelle and when I refused to move to France, she broke it off."

"*She* broke it off? How did you feel about that?" Alexis asked.

"I have to be honest. It was difficult. But I got over it, we put our personal issues aside and eventually were able to maintain a working relationship. What Chantelle and I had, ended at the vineyard property line. Outside of that, we have very little in common," Colton said as he took her hand in his. "There's really not much more to tell." He paused and watched her face.

Alexis looked at their entwined hands. "Just like that? You got over it?"

"That was years ago, Alexis. It wasn't a good match and I knew it in my heart. It wasn't just about who would move to what country," he continued. "We were great in France, but not so much in the real world."

"You were great?" Alexis paused and looked closely at his eyes.

"I didn't mean it quite like that, Alexis. Hey, all of those feelings are in the past." He watched as she took it all in. "Alexis, if I felt about Chantelle like I feel about you, I would have moved to the ends of the Earth for her. It wasn't right and we both knew it. She did us both a favor." He watched her for a few moments in silence. "Are we good?"

"You had something strong if you got engaged. And you still work together, obviously," she stated. "I can't say that doesn't bother me."

"Well, I have to admit that this is a bit of a shock for me, too. She hasn't made a trip here in some time," he sighed. "Hey, I mean it. I'm sorry that I didn't tell you, but there didn't seem to be a reason and well, I'm all about *you*, Alexis." He squeezed her hand. "If it makes any difference, I never proposed to her under the wooden mistletoe. Deep down, I probably knew that she wasn't wooden mistletoe worthy," he smiled. Alexis laughed. "Are we good?" he asked again and waited.

Alexis stared at her feet for what seemed like minutes.

"Don't let her get to you, Alexis. She's a cunning, unpredictable woman who is very good at manipulating others," he added. "There's nothing between us except wines. I promise you that," Colton said as he sat on the table next to her. "You do believe me, don't you?" Alexis was silent. "I'm sorry that Chantelle is acting so badly. I've never seen her behave like that."

"Women can be very possessive, Colton," Alexis said as she studied his face. She paused for a moment, contemplating her next question. "Colton, do you think she's still in love with you?"

He looked down and stared. "I didn't think so, but then I don't seem to know Chantelle like I thought. Her behavior surprised me."

"It's called jealousy." Alexis sat silent for a moment. "I can handle her," she said as she patted his hand and grinned.

"We're good?" he asked.

Alexis put her arms around his neck. "We're good." She gave him a long, affectionate kiss. "Besides, I have something more important to share with you. Let's pour a toast."

"A toast?" he asked.

"Yes. We got approved! The garden and woodshop. We can begin work on Creekside immediately!" She looked at Colton as though she would burst.

"Really? That is *great* news!" He grabbed her and lifted her up, swinging her around. "We did it!" He twirled her around again, put her down and kissed her.

"I *know*!" she laughed.

Colton grabbed one of the bottles, pulled out a glass and splashed wine into it which he handed to Alexis. He picked up his own and clinked them together, raising his in the air. "To Harry and Fifi, our inspiration!"

"Indeed!" she cheered. "To Harry and Fifi!" Alexis raised her glass. Colton leaned in for another long kiss.

"I love you, Alexis," he said, then kissed her again.

Alexis's mouth opened and an inaudible sound came out.

"You can stop looking so surprised, Alexis," he grinned, pulling her toward him again.

"I don't know what to say," she said. They kissed, once again.

"Alexis, I feel like I've known you forever. I hope I'm not being too forward. I mean telling you that I love you and all. Maybe it's crazy, but that's how I feel and I couldn't wait another moment to say it."

She stepped back and leaned against the wall, crossing her arms. "Colton Winters, you are one big surprise. But then I've had quite a few surprises lately that are testing all of my beliefs."

"What *are* your beliefs Alexis Bradford?" he asked as he sat on the table.

"They used to be pretty clear cut, but I'm finding out that I don't know much of anything except," she stepped toward him and took his hand in hers, "that I feel the same way and . . . yes, that seems crazy, and yes, that goes against everything I thought about how things should happen and," she paused as he pulled her close and held her.

"*This* is how things should happen. Let's go with it," he responded. "We have a lot to tackle, and a lot to look forward to!" He placed his hands on her shoulders and pushed her away, looking closely at her face. "This could be the best Christmas ever," he smiled.

"To the best Christmas ever," Alexis said as she picked up her glass and clinked his.

Outside, Chantelle arranged wine boxes in her SUV and walked back into the dark, dirt tasting room to retrieve the last box. She could hear the couple talking in the cavern and cracked the door as she stepped closer to listen. She heard laughter, glasses clink, then silence, and clenched her teeth tightly. Chantelle quietly closed the door and walked out of the room, losing her footing as she carried the wine to her SUV.

"Damn!" she exclaimed seeing that she broke off the heel of her shoe. She continued to walk, limping up and down until she pushed the wine in the back of her vehicle. She closed the trunk, climbed into the driver's seat, and slammed the door. Chantelle stared at the steering wheel, teeth still clenched before finally speeding off, leaving a plume of dust.

Chapter Ten

"Hi there," Alexis said to the elderly woman wearing cargo pants and men's boots standing in front of the many shelves of cat food.

"Hello, young lady. Would you mind helping me place this cat food into my cart? I hope you don't mind, but I'm 90 years old and I'm afraid that I don't have the strength any longer!" she shared. "This is the best bargain, you know. You see, I lost my dog recently and now I feed the stray cats."

"Yes, I know," Alexis spoke. "Do you remember me? I'm the person that spoke to you about the cats . . . and how we both lost our dogs, and feed the strays now?"

The old lady stopped and stared at Alexis, looking her up and down. "Oh, well, I did speak to a woman, but I'm afraid that she didn't look anything like you!" she said, still examining Alexis.

"Sure! I was in a long coat and we talked about not wanting to get another dog and," she started to explain, when the woman interrupted.

"And you were in your pajamas! Oh, yes! I remember!" she said in amazement.

"Oh, well," Alexis said, blushing, "I guess I wasn't hiding it as well as I thought," she frowned.

"Oh yes, the pretty girl in the pajamas." The old lady placed her hand on Alexis's arm and patted it. "Don't worry, my dear. We all have those days. I have to say that this a much better look on you!" she smiled.

"Thank you," Alexis laughed sheepishly. "Unfortunately, I had a lot of those days. Here, let me place that cat food in your cart. Would you like me to help you get it into the car?"

"Oh no, dear. The grocery boy will do that," she said as she watched Alexis lift the bag off the shelf. "You must be in love," she smiled.

Alexis gave her a surprised look.

"Oh, I'm sorry, dear. It's none of my business, but I know that look and I'd say that you are a woman in love. Yes, indeed," she smiled.

"Well, I guess it's confirmed," Alexis grinned.

"Yes, my dear, it shows. Love looks good on you," the woman stated, patting her arm again.

"Thank you," Alexis smiled, with a look of embarrassment. Once again, they connected, but something had changed. Destiny had somehow shifted. "Have a wonderful night."

"And you," she said as she slowly pushed her cart down the aisle. "Love surely is a beautiful look," she mumbled as she continued. "Beautiful indeed."

Alexis stood in the aisle and watched as the woman walked away, and disappeared around the corner. She stood in silence for a moment then quickly made her way to the same aisle. It was empty.

Alexis shook to clear her head and laughed to herself. She remembered what her Grandmother said. "Angels are with you all of the time, Alexis, if you choose to see them." She looked down at her high heels, pretty dress, and cashmere sweater. She was a new person with new possibilities. She stood up straight, took a deep breath and continued shopping then made her way to the checkout.

"Miss, how are you today?" the cashier asked.

"Gertie it's me, Alexis," Alexis answered in surprise.

"Miss Alexis? Oh my! Why of course! I'm so sorry dear! I didn't recognize you without, without your cat food," she replied.

Alexis smiled to herself. "It's fine. I get it."

"Well, with you losing your parents, and dog and all, I can't blame you for . . ." Gertie paused, careful not to be offensive.

"Gertie, it's Okay. I wasn't exactly looking my best. It was rough for a while, but I'm fine," Alexis reassured her.

"Well, you're lookin' lovely, Miss Alexis, mighty lovely," Gertie said as she slid items over the scanner and packed them into bags.

A man got in line behind Alexis and did a double take. He stood tall, sucked in his stomach and smiled. Alexis recognized him from an earlier visit when the glance was not so approving. He gave her a nod. She smiled to herself, grabbed her bags and placed them in her cart. "Thanks, Gertie." Alexis made her way to her car and sat for a moment, smiled, and drove home.

"Knock! Knock!" Jill yelled as she stepped into Alexis's living room.

"Come in!" Alexis shouted back.

Jill walked into the kitchen to find her unpacking her groceries.

"My goodness! Is that a cute dress and high heels I see?" She stepped closer and examined Alexis. "Is that lipstick and mascara you're wearing?"

"Oh stop!" Alexis laughed.

"No, seriously! Who are you?" Jill stepped back and stared, her mouth slightly open.

"I said stop, silly girl!" Alexis laughed again. "Yes, I got dressed today. Yes, I *am* wearing makeup. I even went to the grocery store like this and *not* in my pajamas, I'll have you know." She grinned. "I probably shouldn't tell you this, but even Gertie at the cash register didn't recognize me."

"Well, it's about time. Welcome back, Alexis!" Jill paused. "Is that cashmere?" She touched Alexis's shoulder, stroking the soft sweater.

"Yeah. Do you like it?" Alexis answered.

"Like it? I want to borrow it!" Jill ran her hand down Alexis's arm. "It's so soft!"

"Are you ready for our upcoming work day at Creekside?" Alexis asked.

"Sure am! Got my shovel ready and everything! This is so exciting, what you and Colton are doing. Your Gran must be so proud of you!"

"She is. Jill, between Harry and the prospect of something as simple as being able to pot a few plants, the light in her eyes is back," Alexis placed the last item in the refrigerator.

"I think it's awesome and I'm looking forward to being a part of it," Jill said and paused. "Any chance Jackson will be there?"

"Ah, she's sweet on Jackson! He *is* pretty cute. Yes, he'll be there."

"Oh good!" Jill got excited. "That adorable southern charm just got to me. I'd better wear my best farmer dungarees!"

Alexis laughed loudly. "Dungarees? What the heck? You're so funny."

"It's so good to see you laugh, Alex." Jill hugged her then pulled items from the grocery bags and placed them in various cupboards. "So, hot shot, what's new?"

"Well, I hate to even bring this up," Alexis grinned.

"Uh oh. This sounds serious. Hey, I'm your wing man, remember? Out with it."

Alexis paused, then continued. "Just when everything seemed so right, I got a reality check. I was at the vineyards yesterday and there was a surprise visit."

"Yes?" Jill's interest peaked.

"From a woman. Apparently, Colton was engaged once," Alexis continued with a blank face.

"Seriously? Wow. How did you find that out?" Jill asked, pulling a grape out of a bag and placing it in her mouth.

"She actually introduced herself as his fiancé! Can you believe that?"

"She's his fiancé? What?" Jill froze.

"Yeah. Crazy, huh? Colton corrected her. She was his 'former' fiancé, but can you believe the guts it took to say that? I smell trouble."

Alexis pursed her lips. "Apparently, she reps her family's French vineyard and Winters collaborates with them," she shared.

"Ohhh, right! The trips to France! Geez, Alexis. You actually met her?" Jill shoved another grape in her mouth.

"Yes, and she's beautiful. It sent shock waves to my core. Colton was fine, but Chantelle . . . that's her name . . . seemed to have a real interest in him."

"She's pretty? What was she like?" Jill was riveted.

"She's pretty alright. Legs up to her neck and by her blatant behavior, I think she's still interested in Colton." She looked at Jill, feeling uncomfortable at having said it and leaned against the counter.

"Do you think she's still in love with him?" Jill asked.

"I don't know, but let's just say that I think that I've spurred Chantelle's competitive spirit," Alexis responded.

"Typical," Jill said, as she situated herself. "As soon as another woman is in the picture, the old jealousy kicks in and the little kitten turns into a lioness. I wouldn't worry about it. Colton is totally in love with you."

"You think so?" Alexis asked, carefully watching Jill.

"Why Alexis Bradford, it's not like you to be insecure!"

"Am I being insecure? I thought I was just in love," Alexis grinned.

"Same thing. And honey, you're in love! That's wonderful!" Jill hugged Alexis. "I know how scary that can be. You know, you're feeling all good and powerful and then some guy comes into your life and we turn into mush! I know. Remember Brad Kemp?" Jill crinkled her nose.

"Oh, yes. Good old Brad," Alexis smirked and crossed her arms.

"Yeah, good ol' Brad is right. I acted like a school girl around him. He made me downright nervous! All that 'Jill 'confidence' went right out the window."

Alexis let out a big sigh. "Yeah, you just described it perfectly, I'm afraid. It's frightening. I feel like I don't have control anymore."

"Is that a bad thing?" Jill smiled. "Really, *is* that so bad? I mean, it's totally worth it, don't you think? Colton's a great guy." She paused. "Alexis, do you think he's the one?"

Alexis turned and looked at her with a serious expression. "Yeah, I do." She felt her face flush. "And then this woman shows up and my world feels so unsure again."

"That's understandable." Jill smiled. "You have to get your sea legs back, that's all. Are you along for the ride? I mean, you know that there are no guarantees. Are you willing to see where it takes you?"

Alexis paused and thought. "It's too late to quit now. Yeah, I'm in."

"Well, welcome back Alexis Bradford!" Jill laughed and hugged her. "I'm proud of you! Don't worry about Chantelle. She's old news. Besides, I'm sure she'll be heading back to France, right?"

"Yeah, I guess," Alexis responded.

"Hey, are you sure you're Okay?" Jill asked.

"Yeah. Don't worry about me," Alexis squeezed Jill's arm. "It's just tough to stick my toe back in the water."

"Alexis, you're fabulous! If Colton wanted Frenchie, he would have married her when he had the chance!"

"That's just it. She broke up with him. He was heartbroken," Alexis looked intently at Jill.

"Oh," Jill said and paused, not knowing what to say next. "Well, there's nothing that you can do, right? Colton adores you and until you have proof of anything else, I say we keep our heads held high and forge ahead." Jill paused and smiled. "Let's focus on getting Creekside built out."

"Deal," Alexis agreed.

Jill turned and started to walk out of the kitchen then stopped. "And, Alex, forget about Frenchie. Put the blinders on and be your fabulous self."

"Thanks, my friend," Alexis smiled.

"I'll see you at Creekside," she said as she turned to leave. "You call me if you need anything!" she shouted before closing the door.

Alexis finished putting her groceries away before walking into her living room where she sat on the sofa. She sighed, pulled off her high heels and rubbed her feet.

Chapter Eleven

"Chantelle, you'll be working with Jackson from now on," Colton said as he stood behind the counter of the winery's main tasting area, unpacking bottles of wine.

Jackson entered the room with a box and placed it on the counter before Colton. "Last one."

"Jackson, you of course know Chantelle," Colton continued. "You and Chantelle will be coordinating the wine selection and purchases."

"Jackson? Zees name, is zees a first name?" Chantelle asked sarcastically as she eyed him up and down.

"Yes, Ma'am. I mean no Ma'am. It's Thomas Jackson Wentworth Ma'am, but I go by Jackson," he said loudly and with great pride.

"We have met before," Chantelle rudely stated as she turned slightly away, still examining him out of the corner of her eye.

"We sure have Ma'am! When you and Colton here got engaged, I was at yer' celebration party here at the vineyards! I see you all the time when you visit us here in the U.S.," he happily announced, pulling up his jeans and pushing his hands deep into his pockets.

"Jackson, she's being a smart aleck. Chantelle, you know Jackson. You see him every time you visit these vineyards, so please don't pretend," Colton said, looking somewhat annoyed at her games.

"Well, sometimes I do *not* remember," Chantelle said as she crossed her arms and looked away. "I thought he was zees stock boy."

"Jackson here is my cousin," Colton reminded her. "He's been working here for quite some time now, which you are well aware of."

Chantelle, quickly turned toward Jackson. "Well!" She looked at him, once again, from head to toe. "If I must, then I will comply with zees. Does zees person know anything about wines?"

"Yes Ma'am! Colton here, well, he's taught me everything I know!" Jackson said as he slapped Colton on the back. "I'm perty good at tastin' and all. You won't have to worry about ol' Jackson here. I can keep up with ya'll, including those fancy French wines," he said, nodding his head confidently.

"You won't be disappointed," Colton assured her.

Chantelle turned toward Colton. "So, you are so beezy that you have no time for me? You push Chantelle off on someone else? Is zees woman you are seeing jealous of me?"

"No, Chantelle. Alexis is not jealous. You have the prize in that department. And, yes, you will be working with Jackson. It's not an option," Colton said, not losing eye contact with her.

She turned toward Jackson and reluctantly extended her hand. "Then I will work with you Mr. Jackson, Colton's cousin."

"Just Jackson Ma'am," he said giving her a vigorous handshake.

"Please, do not address me wis zees 'Ma'am'," she said frowning. "It eez so. . . so, *old*."

"Sure, Miss Chantelle, Ma'am. I mean, Chantelle. There's no way anyone would think you are old! Well, yer' still a young filly!" Jackson turned toward Colton. "Well, I best be takin' care of the inventory." Chantelle managed a slight smile as she continued to watch him.

"Sure. Thanks, Jackson I'll meet up with you later," Colton said, patting him on the back.

Jackson left the room, with big strides, shaking his head and laughing to himself. "Heh, heh! Miss Chantelle! That is one funny gal! Heh heh!"

Chantelle stared him down. "He looks more like your brother, but stupeed."

"I assure you that Jackson is far from stupid."

"But he is not so, as you would say, 'clever,'" she commented.

"Oh, don't let that southern drawl fool you. Ol' Jackson there is a university graduate in enology and viticulture." Colton saw the blank look on Chantelle's face. "The study of winemaking, vine-growing and grape-harvesting."

"I know what zees is! My family owns a vineyard, remember? Oh!" she exclaimed in frustration.

"Jackson brings a lot to the table and Dad and I have learned a lot from him," Colton stated.

"He is young? No?" Chantelle asked.

"Not so young. My age. Older than you," Colton responded, watching her. "Are you worried that I left you with a moron?" he said with a frown.

Chantelle gasped in an over exaggerated manner. "I would not say such a thing! Not about your brother, Colton." She placed her hand on his shoulder and stroked his arm affectionately.

"He's my cousin, Chantelle," Colton frowned. "You don't have to like him. Just *try* to be nice to him, will you?" He pulled his arm away.

"Colton," she batted her eyes at him. "Why do you pull away? You must not feel fear, no?"

"I'm not afraid of you, Chantelle. I just want to make sure that you understand our relationship," he said looking her straight in the eyes.

"Of course! We share za' wine, we choose za' wine, it is good, no?" she smiled in a flirtatious manner.

"Yes, it is good. Now can you please go talk to Jackson? *You* may learn something from *him*." He turned and picked up a box of wine and headed in the opposite direction.

"Colton!" she exclaimed. "Please." Colton turned back around. Chantelle appeared serious and deflated.

"What Chantelle? What is it now?" he asked.

She walked to him and looked into his eyes. "I know eet has been a long time since we . . . we were together. But," she paused and sighed. "We were in love, my Colton." She paused again and a look of sincerity came over her. "Eet was good, yes?" Colton didn't respond.

"Zees feelings have never gone for me. I think that I made . . . I made a meestake."

"You made a mistake about what, Chantelle?" Colton asked with a sarcastic look on his face.

"You think I make zees up?" she gasped, seeming offended.

"I don't know, Chantelle. I really don't. Why, all of a sudden, is this coming up? It's been years and now you decide that you made a mistake? Is that why you're here? I don't believe it. I think you broke another heart and now you're back to claim your old turf. I think that you can't stand not being the center of attention. Perhaps you're just a little jealous to know that Alexis is now the focus of mine."

"No! Zees is not true! I am here to taste za wines, of course and work with za Winters winery. It eez my job, of course. Wis zees new project at za old person's home, I am staying here longer to help." She examined his face, knowing that he was not convinced. "Yes, it is true that zees woman has sparked some, some jealousy in me. And I asked myself 'why?' Why do I feel zees way? And I know eet eez my feelings for you." She stared at Colton, waiting for a response.

"Chantelle, you can't expect me to believe that," he frowned.

"Yes? Zees is so ridiculous to you? I think you know that we belong together. Za timing, it was not good before." She batted her eyes and looked back into his. "Yes, I was za selfeesh leetle girl, wanting my way. Now, I know eet was wrong. Zat I lost za most importeent person in my life." She paused and placed her arm on his shoulder. "Colton, I am za woman you must be with. You once proposed. I know you felt zat I was special. We were meant to be togezer. You and I, we are za beautiful couple. Our families, zay go togezer so perfectly. You know zees is true." She waited for his response.

"Once it was, Chantelle. Once it was." He took her hand in his and patted it. "I was proud to propose to you. That was another time. It is no longer true. I'm sorry." He patted her hand again and placed it at her side. "There is someone out there for you. You'll find him. For now, you need to give up this idea and I don't want you to speak to anyone about this. Do I have your word?"

Chantelle's face fell and she pushed her bottom lip out. "You will think about zees, no?"

"No," he responded.

"Not a leetle beet?" Chantelle cocked her head to one side and moved closer to him. "Just for me? Your leetle Chan-ee?" She took both of her hands and placed them on his chest. "Zees girl, she is a writer? What does she know about za wines. We share za love of wines. Do you remember za time we made love in za orchards?" She kissed his cheek and brushed her body against his.

"Yes, Chantelle. I remember." He grinned. "You are something Chan-ee. You certainly are something," he said, shaking his head.

Chantelle grinned, pleased that she had somehow gotten through to him when he suddenly took both of her shoulders and pushed her back a step.

"Now go find Jackson."

She folded her arms, gave a big sigh and spun around before heading out the door. Colton turned and stared out the window over the orchards, deep in thought.

Chapter Twelve

The town rallied as supplies, workers, and food arrived at Creekside. Each day, Eileen set up a table with coffee and pies. Andy and his contractors donated their skills and others showed up with tools, and any items that they could contribute. Even the local ladies came to lend a hand in the garden. The Creekside project was slowly becoming a reality.

"Hey!" Alexis waved at the volunteers as she stepped out of her car. The Creekside warehouse doors were open wide. Inside, Colton and Jackson along with several other men were moving heavy equipment and strategically placing it. Others were hammering and sawing pieces of wood.

Colton looked up. "Hi there!" He waved at Alexis.

Jill pulled in the parking area directly behind her. "Wait for me!" she shouted as she stepped out of her car and made her way toward the warehouse.

"Welcome ladies!" Jackson waved.

The women stepped into the building. "It's really coming along," Alexis commented as she looked around the large space. The room was filled with people working, drills and saws buzzing, and chatter as they worked on various projects.

"We've had a lot of help!" Colton said as he looked around at the work tables and equipment.

"I can't wait to see the look on Harry's and Fifi's faces," Alexis said.

"We'll be finished just in time for the volunteer's Barn Dance this weekend at the vineyards," Colton shared.

"We're all looking forward to that," Alexis stated.

"Well, it's the least we can do for them. They've worked really hard."

"I know you said that everything is all prepared, but isn't there something I can do to help?"

"Nothing," a voice piped in. Chantelle stood behind Alexis. "Za details are already handled." She turned toward Colton. "Colton? May I speak wiz you?"

Colton's expression turned serious and he appeared to be nervous. "Can it wait?" he asked.

"No." She took his arm and pulled him toward the warehouse doors.

Alexis stood and stared as Colton, embarrassed, looked back at her. "I'll talk to you later," he said as he disappeared outside, with Chantelle dragging him.

"How's it going?" Jill asked Jackson as she stepped closer and leaned on a piece of equipment he was working on.

"Right well, Ma'am! Right well," he smiled. "I reckon we'll have it lookin' all professional and ready for these old folks to start buildin' things!"

"Well, I reckon you're right," Jill said as she batted her eye lashes. "Will you be goin' to the Barn Dance this weekend?"

"Sure will. It's at the Winters Vineyards, and I'm in charge of the barbeque," he answered.

"Well then I'll bet it will be the best barbeque!" Jill batted her eyes again. "May I assist with the event?"

"I reckon that you could help out with pourin' some wines. But, most of all just come and have some fun!" he smiled.

"Oh, I certainly will!" she said, leaning closer as Jackson continued to work.

"Ah hem! Jill, may I speak with you for a moment," Alexis said as she walked to the couple. She turned toward Jackson. "Jackson, will you excuse us? My friend and I have a garden that awaits our attention."

"Ma'am, you go right on ahead!" he said with a big smile.

"Oh, right," Jill stood straight and frowned. She leaned closer to Jackson. "I guess I'd better get to diggin' in that garden!" she smiled. "Feel free to come by and visit," she added, taking on a slight southern accent.

"Right will," Jackson said as he took off his baseball cap. "But I think I'll be tied up here for a good piece of the day."

Alexis smiled. "Thank you, Jackson. We'll let you get back to work." She grabbed Jill's arm and lead her away from the work area and outside where Chantelle and Colton were nowhere to be found.

"What? I was making headway!" Jill stated reluctantly. "You interrupted weeks of flirting progress." She watched Alexis who intently viewed the surroundings. "What are you looking for?"

"Not what, but who. Chantelle. And Colton. She's up to it again," Alexis shared as she continued to stare into the distance.

"Up to what?" Jill asked.

"Her usual antics," Alexis responded. "She pulled Colton away to have another private conversation." Alexis continued to look around the building and into the distance but saw nothing. "Something is going on."

"What are you insinuating?" Jill paused.

Alexis turned and examined her face. "You mean do I think that they are having an affair? No! I mean, I don't know what's happening. I mean, no, of course they aren't having an affair. But, she's still here and she's still clinging to him every moment she gets!" She was surprised at her own words. "Wow, I sound so insecure!"

"I can't blame you, Alexis. I thought she was supposed to go back to France."

"Yeah, so did I, but she managed to stay and help with this project. I think it was an excuse to spend time with Colton," Alexis stated. "I haven't seen her lift a finger, either! She just hangs out in the work area, wherever Colton is, and she's staying at the vineyards!"

"Well, she's going to have to go back soon, right? She can't stay here forever," Jill asked. "And you and Colton are good, right?"

Alexis stared at her for a moment and sighed. "He's been distant, like he has something on his mind."

"Alexis, don't worry about it. There's a lot going on with the Creekside project, and ol' Frenchie yanking on Colton every chance she gets. He has a lot to handle with this and running the vineyards."

"And the woodshop. He's been working on my mantle," Alexis responded.

"Oh right. I forgot about that. See? He has a lot to handle. Don't worry. You focus on Colton and I'll keep my eye on Frenchie."

"You're right," Alexis said and managed a smile. "Come on. I'm just getting myself worked up. Let's take a break and visit my Gran."

"You mean Michael?" Jill asked excitedly.

"I mean Gran." Alexis grabbed Jill's hand and dragged her down a path and into the home. The women made their way to her Grandmother's room.

"Grandmother, we're here!" Alexis exclaimed after knocking.

"Well, hello there!" Gran said excitedly as she sat in a chair, watching television. "How is my darling angel?" She put both arms out, inviting a hug.

"If you're referring to me, your angel is just fine. How is my beautiful Grandmother?" Alexis asked as she approached and gave her a big hug. "You remember Jill?"

"Of course, I do!" Gran smiled and stretched her arms out again for a hug.

Jill reciprocated. "Granny B, it's so good to see you!"

"Well, I hear you young ladies are here to finish that lovely garden for us old folks!" she laughed.

"Well, we're going to do our best!" Jill responded.

"I'm grateful to you girls, and I know that Harry is so excited about getting into that workshop." Gran grabbed Alexis's hand. "All of the residents are excited. This is a good thing you're doing, Alexis. More than you know."

Alexis squeezed her hand and smiled. "I think I do know, Gran. Now, how are you?"

"Quite well, my dear. Quite well. That Harry has been a blessing and such a good friend," she beamed. "And it was fate that you were to meet young Colton! We're lucky ladies, us Bradford women!"

"That we are!" Alexis agreed looking away. "Well, I just wanted to check in on you and make sure everything is set for the event. Jill and I are going to get busy in that garden. Do you have your dress all ready for the ribbon cutting ceremony? You know it's in just a few days, right?"

"Oh yes. Mabel helped me try it on and got it all pressed!" Gran stated with excitement.

"Perfect," Alexis said, giving her a kiss on the forehead. "I'll be here early to help get you all pretty." Jill and Alexis turned to leave.

"Alexis!" Gran said as they began to exit. "Is everything Okay my dear?"

"Yes, Gran, why?" Alexis asked.

"Oh, a mother hen knows when something isn't quite right with her little chick." She paused and examined Alexis. "Alexis, talk to your Grand Mama. Come back here and sit down."

Alexis walked back into the room and sat on the bed.

"Is it love my dear? Is it that young man?" Gran said with a peaceful expression.

"Oh, Gran, you don't want to hear this," Alexis stated. "It's nothing."

"Now I may be an old woman, but I have some experience in the department of love. What is it that is bothering your soul?" she asked.

Alexis looked at Jill who nodded and sighed. "I guess I just don't understand men," she grinned.

Her Grandmother laughed loudly. "And they say women are hard to figure out! Yes, we have our moments, but men, well they have a way of confusing us, sometimes by simply saying nothing!"

"And I'm feeling so vulnerable. I don't know what to do! Gran, there's this woman that Colton used to love. She works with him and she's here from France," Alexis became serious. "In fact, she's stayed on much longer than she was supposed to, and,"

"And she's stirring the pot!" Gran squinted her eyes and raised an eyebrow.

"You could say that," Jill said.

"Uh huh. Women can be clever manipulators to get what they want, but in the end the truth wins," Gran shared.

"I know. Maybe I don't want to believe what the truth is right now," Alexis said giving Jill a look of concern.

"Everything always happens for the best," Gran continued. "You know to always go with your heart, but that doesn't assure that things will always turn out as you would like them to. Sometimes the best outcome is learning a life lesson, painful as it may be."

"Gran, is that another message from Michael?" Alexis asked.

"Oh no, dear. This is advice from me," her Gran smiled. "I know it's difficult when feelings are involved, but keep your chin up and know that fate will take its course. Stay strong little chick."

"Fate," Alexis frowned. "I know a thing or two about fate." She stood. "Thank you, Gran. We'd better get ourselves out to that garden now. I love you," Alexis said.

"Take care of my girl," Gran said to Jill. Jill reached out and squeezed her hand.

"You know I will," Jill assured her. The two friends left the room.

"Is it that obvious?" Alexis asked.

"Well, maybe not to most people, but your Gran knows you well," Jill answered. "I agree with her. The truth always wins, Alexis."

"Does it? There's nothing that can be done. Let's get into some dirt and enjoy this beautiful day," Alexis said.

The two made their way to the garden area where over a dozen volunteers had gathered, digging, hauling patio stones and garden pieces. A backhoe was clearing areas for planting. Wide paths were created with retreats along the way including sitting benches and bird baths. A wheelchair friendly potting area was almost complete.

"Oh, my gosh," Alexis said quietly as they stood and watched the organized chaos.

Jill placed her arm around Alexis. "This is all because of you."

"This is beyond me," Alexis responded as her eyes welled up with tears. "This is the result of good, caring people."

"And a lot of love," Jill added. They both stood for a moment. "Well, I guess I'd better get those gloves on and pitch in."

"Yeah, let's get in there," Alexis said as she pulled her gloves out of a back pocket. "Hey everyone!" she shouted to the volunteers who responded with greetings.

The two joined in the digging and chatted excitedly with the townspeople as the garden was slowly completed with each hour that passed.

Lunch time came and went and the crews worked until darkness set in. It was the final day of work and the volunteers eventually congregated in the warehouse for refreshments before slowly heading out. Colton and Alexis thanked each as they packed up equipment and tools, loaded trucks and left the grounds.

"I'd say this was an enormous success," Alexis said as she waved to the last volunteer.

"Alexis," Colton began, as he walked to her with a look of reluctance. "Can I speak with you? There's something that I need to tell you."

"Of course," Alexis said, giving Jill a quick glance across the room.

"Hey, Alexis!" Jill shouted. "I'm going to go wash up and get out of these dirty clothes. I'll see you back home." She winked and left.

The two were now alone in the warehouse. "I want to apologize for being so distant." He paused, looked at the floor then walked to a large, wooden table and leaned against it. "I've just had a lot on my mind."

Alexis walked to him and placed her hand on his arm. "Colton, you know you can always talk to me, about *anything*." She waited for his response.

He looked at her and smiled. "I know." He took her hand in his. "You know I care very much for you, don't you?"

"Well, yes. And I feel the same," she managed to put on a smile.

"We've really taken on a lot," he said and patted her hand. "All in a very short period of time."

"That's for sure," Alexis agreed, anxious to hear more.

"These past few weeks, well, we've accomplished a lot too," he looked deep into her eyes. "So much has transpired along the way," he continued when Chantelle suddenly marched into the warehouse in her usual heels and tight dress.

"Colton?" she blurted. "Jackson has loaded the truck. We must get back to za vineyards. There is much to do!" She turned and marched out.

Alexis looked at Colton. "She's still staying at the vineyards?"

"Well, yeah. I thought you knew that," he said. "I mean, it didn't make sense since we have a guest house and all. There's so much going on and, well, she's been real helpful."

"Oh, well. I mean that's fine. It's just a surprise." Alexis's face flushed.

"Listen, if it's Okay with you, Jackson and I are going to stop by and install the mantel tomorrow. I think you're going to love it."

This was not the time or place to push him for more. "Tomorrow would be great," she answered and kissed him. She walked to the exit and turned. "Colton?" He looked up at her as he began to pack his tool kit. "Was there something you wanted to tell me?"

"Well, nothing much. It can wait." He smiled.

"Sure. I'll see you tomorrow." Alexis made her way to her car. Sitting in a truck, waiting for Colton were Chantelle and Jackson, watching her. She reluctantly waved and drove home.

Chapter Thirteen

"Alexis!" Colton shouted as he opened the front door of the mountain house. "We're here!" He and Jackson entered carrying the new mantel. They walked into the living room, one on each end of the heavy piece of wood as Alexis appeared from the hallway.

"Hey there! Come in! I laid out a sheet," she said pointing to the space in front of the fireplace. "You can set it down there."

"Great," Colton responded as they rested it on the floor as instructed. "Excited?"

"I am!" Alexis responded as she examined the wood. "This is even better than I imagined." She ran her hand over it. "It's beautiful. You did a great job."

There was a knock on the door and Alexis opened it to find Andy standing in front of her with a big smile. "Andy, come in. The mantel just arrived."

Andy's tool belt clanked as he entered and greeted the two men. "That's a mighty fine piece of wood. Miss Alexis, this is somethin' to be proud to display in this nice home of yours!"

"It is, Andy." Alexis answered as she watched them get busy measuring and marking the wall.

Colton and Jackson began to drill holes and secure anchors. "Oh, darn. I forgot the set of drill bits. Alexis, there's a tool bag in the back of the truck. Can you go out and rifle through it to find them? We'll need smaller holes on the underside," Colton requested.

"Sure," Alexis agreed, then made her way out to the driveway. She crawled in the back seat where she found the leather tool pouch and pushed several screwdrivers aside, feeling for the small case of drill bits. Unable to see anything, she pulled the pouch closer to the door to gain more light. As she moved the tools, a letter fell out from a side pocket and onto the driveway. She picked it up. On the outside was written, 'My Love.'

Alexis stood and stared at the letter. Should she place it back in the pouch or read it? Was this a violation of trust? A demonstration of her insecurity? Of course, it was. She opened it.

"My Love, I know that this is a very uncomfortable situation and that this is truly a surprise, our feelings. I do not claim that I deserve to be a part of the Winters family. Perhaps in time, I will be accepted and forgiven for my past behavior. But, this is fate that I am back and that we have connected. You cannot deny that we are meant to be together, although I know you are trying. I know that you would feel unfaithful by declaring our love, but it is meant to be. It is not random nor coincidence that I have returned to the U.S. We can no longer hide this love and it is time to reveal it to the world. I will not wait. I will be returning to France shortly and I demand that you make our engagement announcement before I leave. We must make plans immediately for me to come back to where I truly belong, Winters Vineyards, and with you. I love you completely, Chantelle"

Alexis felt her heart palpitate and her breath quicken. She pushed the letter back into the envelope and into the tool pouch before grabbing the drill bits. She closed the truck door and slowly made her way back to the house. Thoughts raced through her mind. Chantelle was back, was on a mission to capture Colton's heart, and now it was confirmed. She could hardly breathe and the blood drained out of her face.

She stepped into the house and stood in the entrance watching the men hoist the mantel up and put it in place. She stared, now thoughtless.

"Good timing! Did you have a problem finding it?" Colton asked as he looked at Alexis. "You Okay?"

Alexis continued to stare. "Uh, yeah." She paused. "Yeah, I'm fine." She walked to Colton and handed him the drill bits.

"Thanks! I just need to secure it with a few small screws and we're good to go. What do you think? Beautiful?" he asked.

"Uh, yeah. Yeah, it's beautiful," Alexis said, forcing herself to speak.

Colton took out a bit and pushed it into the drill head, tightening it. He looked back at Alexis. "Hey," he said, touching her shoulder. "What's wrong?"

Alexis looked up at him. "Oh, it's nothing. I think I ate something that didn't sit right with me. I'll be Okay," she answered.

"You sure?" he asked. "You look a little pale."

"No, I'm fine. Really," she insisted, trying to regain her composure.

"If you say so." Colton stepped back and looked at the mantel. "Perfect." He handed the drill to Jackson. "Go ahead and put the screws in place."

Jackson got busy drilling the small screws on the bottom while Andy assisted.

Colton grabbed Alexis's hand and walked her into the kitchen. "Anyone want a cup of coffee?" he asked the men, who were still busy working. They both accepted the offer. Colton began to prepare a pot of coffee as Alexis continued to stand and stare like a zombie. "Did you get a phone call or something?" he asked.

"No. I just . . . I must be coming down with something," she answered.

"Well, you'd better take care of yourself. The Creekside Ribbon Cutting is in a couple of days and the Barn Dance is tomorrow."

"I'll be fine," she answered as she opened a cupboard and retrieved several coffee cups. She pulled them out and watched Colton prepare the pot of coffee. "Colton," she said as she leaned against the counter. "Is everything good with you?"

"Yeah. It's going great," he responded. "Why?"

"I don't know. You seem a little distant lately, like something's on your mind." She waited and watched.

Colton continued to prepare the coffee and smiled, without looking at her. "Well, like I shared with you. We've just taken on a lot in a short period of time. I think it's just taken its toll on me. Obvious, huh?"

"Yeah, pretty much. Care to divulge?" Alexis asked.

"Nothing that I want to bother you with. Not before the ceremony," he said and looked at her. "It's going to be a special day and I don't want anything to spoil it."

"What could spoil it?" she asked, taking a deep breath.

"Nothing." He finished pouring the water into the coffee maker. "I just have a lot on my mind."

"Where's that coffee?" Jackson shouted as he stepped back and stared at the mantle. "Looks straight to me," he said. Andy nodded in agreement.

"Coming!" Colton answered. "Do you have any cream?" he asked Alexis.

"Yeah. I have a fresh container in the fridge." She walked to the refrigerator as she continued to watch Colton who stared at the coffee dribbling into the pot. "Go on, Colton. I'll take care of it."

"Great. Thanks," he said and joined the men in the living room.

Alexis watched him as the men chatted and cleaned up their tools. They gladly accepted the coffee and discussed their handiwork, packed up and departed.

Chapter Fourteen

"Ya hoo! Welcome everybody! Attention!" Jackson shouted as he stood on the stage in the Winters Barn. "Welcome to the Creekside Project Volunteer Party!" Men and women, dressed in jeans, boots and cowboy hats laughed and chatted with one another as they lined up at tables loaded with wine and other libations. "It's the Winter's way of saying 'thank you' for all of you who helped to make some really nice, old people happy!" Colton who joined him on the stage grabbed the microphone as the crowd laughed.

"Ah hem!" Colton smiled. "What Jackson is trying to say is that we're mighty grateful to y'all for all of the work that you've put into making dreams come true. In two days, we'll have the ribbon cutting ceremony and I hope y'all will attend. But tonight, is for you. Help yourselves to the tables of Winters wines and out back, Jackson is cooking up a mean barbeque. Have fun and let's get some barn dancin' going!" he shouted as the crowd whooped and clapped.

A country band stationed behind Colton on the stage started playing. Several couples stepped into the center of the barn and began to dance. Others sat on bales of hay, eating and drinking.

"Alexis, look at me," Jill said as she pulled Alexis to a corner in the barn. "This could go one of several ways." She stopped and stared, then took a deep breath. "Listen, it's not like me to say this. I haven't exactly been such a trusting person in my past relationships and I'm learning. It's just that I was thinking about what your Gran said and Michael's message." Alexis frowned. "Yeah, I know, it all seems a bit whacky, but that message about the mistletoe, and fork in the road . . . it can't be a random coincidence." Jill took Alexis's hands in hers.

"Michael said to 'go with your heart' and I agree. What does your heart tell you, Alexis?"

Alexis looked at the ground, fighting off tears. "I don't know."

"Are you sure? Somehow I think that you *do* know." Jill paused and stared at Alexis who was still looking down. "Search your heart, Alexis. What do you truly feel?"

Alexis looked up, tears streaming down her cheeks. "I want to believe. I want to trust him," she answered.

"And?" Jill asked.

Alexis thought for a moment. "I think that he feels the same way that I do." She looked at Jill with a serious expression. "But, Jill, the note told the truth. I can't ignore what I read."

"Your Gran was right. Go with your heart. It doesn't mean things will turn out as you want them to, but this is the best decision, don't you think? You just have to trust. He doesn't know that you saw that note. Alexis, you have nothing to lose," Jill said as she squeezed Alexis's hands. "Now wipe those tears and go out there and dance with that man. You'll find out the truth soon enough." Jill leaned forward and hugged her.

"You think so?" Alexis managed a smile.

"Like your Gran said, 'the truth always comes out' and I trust your Gran. Now put a smile on your face and get out there." She nudged Alexis.

"Alright, but you'd better not go far. I may need some moral support," Alexis said as she wiped a tear on her sleeve. She stood up straight and took a few steps before looking back at Jill who motioned her to continue.

"Hey," Alexis said as she made her way to Colton who was still standing on the stage.

"Hey," Colton smiled and hopped off. "You ready to two-step?"

"Sure," Alexis said as he took her hand.

The couple made their way to the dance area and joined in a

growing crowd that shuffled and twirled. Music and laughter filled the room. Garden lights strung along the interior of the barn created a warm glow. The air was permeated with the smell of smoky barbeque.

"Having fun?" Colton asked as he twirled Alexis.

"Yeah. This is a nice event," Alexis forced a smile.

"You ready for the big ceremony? Harry is anxious to get into that workshop," he smiled.

"Yeah. It's going to be great," Alexis responded with her best effort to sound enthusiastic.

"You still tired?" Colton asked, noticing her lack of energy.

"I am," Alexis answered as Colton twirled her again.

"Well, all of our hard work is finished. You'll be able to get some rest," he said as they two-stepped around the dance floor.

On the side, arms folded, watching them intently stood Chantelle. Colton caught her staring and suddenly became uncomfortable. "Want to grab a glass of wine?" he asked as he took Alexis's hand and walked her off the floor.

"Sure," she answered, as she looked back at Chantelle who still stood, staring.

The couple walked to a table where Colton poured them both a glass of wine. Still, Chantelle watched them. "Come on, let's step outside to get some fresh air," Colton suggested.

Outside, guests were seated at picnic tables eating barbeque and visiting. Jackson was busy at the smoky grill serving the now growing line of people.

"Over here," Colton said, pulling her away from the crowd. "There's something that I want to talk to you about." They walked to the side of the barn where only a string of lights revealed the way.

Colton stopped and put one hand into his jeans pocket. He took a sip of wine and paused, then looked up at the sky. "Beautiful night, isn't it?" he commented.

Alexis took a deep breath and a sip of wine. "It is." She paused and watched him as he continued to gaze at the sky. "What's up, Colton?"

"Life is funny, isn't it?" He looked at Alexis with a sad smile. "It's full of surprises."

"It is," Alexis said, as she felt a flush of heat rushing up her body and making its way to her neck. "What is it, Colton? What do you need to tell me?" She held her breath.

"I'm not going to beat around the bush. It's about Chantelle," he looked at her with a serious, pained expression.

"What about her?" Alexis asked as she sat down at a picnic table to steady herself.

"There is a reason why she's stayed over for so long. I think it's pretty obvious that she didn't stay because she cares about helping old people with their garden!" he smiled.

"Yeah, I figured that much," Alexis managed a smile.

"Something very unexpected and very surprising has happened. I've hesitated to tell you because, well, because I've been trying to process all of it myself." He paused and stood in front of her.

"Colton, I think I know what you're about to say," Alexis said.

"No, I don't think you do, actually," he continued. "This is going to take you by surprise, Alexis."

Colton suddenly looked into the distance. Alexis turned to see what caught his attention. Coming out of the barn was Chantelle who looked around at the crowd until she finally spotted the couple. She stood tall and with a determined walk, made her way toward them.

"Mon Amour! She must know!" Chantelle insisted as she walked up to them.

"Chantelle, what are you doing?" Colton asked, raising his voice. "You need to leave. I can handle this."

"There is no more time," Chantelle folded her arms. "She needs to know now!" She turned abruptly and marched back to the barn and inside.

The two stood in silence as they watched her exit.

"Colton, I know what's going on," Alexis said, her hands now trembling.

"You know?" Colton blurted out.

"It was pretty obvious, Colton, from the day she arrived." Alexis's heart was racing.

"Well, it may have been obvious to you, but not to me!" he replied. "It wasn't planned or anything!" He paused. "No one is happy about this, least of all me. I thought she was out of my life for good." He nervously paced back and forth. "There is something else you need to know, Alexis," he reluctantly continued. "The engagement, well, it's going to be announced tonight."

"You can't be serious!" Alexis gasped.

"It's the only way Chantelle can stay in the country. I know it's terrible timing and my family is not happy about it." He watched as Alexis stood silent, her breathing quickened.

"The timing is terrible? That's all you can say?" Alexis took a step back. "I, I can't think straight. The opening is tomorrow night, Colton. We need to just get through this."

"Look, you know how much I care for you. I never wanted to keep secrets from you. I didn't want to ruin all of this. I didn't mean to upset you, Alexis but it's out of my control! Alexis, Chantelle, well, she's not such a bad person. She really isn't. Let's not let this ruin anything, Okay?"

"Ruin anything? Oh, right. We wouldn't want to ruin the day for Chantelle!"

"Alexis, please," Colton said.

"So, you were just going to announce this and surprise me? In front of everyone?"

"Well, not exactly. I was going to talk to you beforehand, to get your blessing," he said.

"My blessing? You can't be serious! Wow, this is all too much," Alexis said as she turned to leave.

"Alexis! Wait! I'm sorry!" Colton exclaimed as he watched her run back into the barn.

"What happened?" Jackson suddenly appeared and stood behind Colton. "You told her?"

"I did, but she already knew," Colton said. "And Chantelle just couldn't wait to show off."

"Colton, you found the love of your life. Alexis will understand. She'll get over it," Jackson assured him.

"Will she?" Colton asked and looked at him. "I need to get back inside." He quickly walked away. Jackson stood and watched him.

"Get over here," Alexis said as she walked to Jill and grabbed her arm, quickly heading to the barn exit.

"Where are we going? What happened? You're hurting my arm!" Jill stopped abruptly. "Alexis, tell me, what's going on."

"It's exactly what I thought. The letter, the feelings between them, all of it. It's true. I gave it a chance and now I know. It's over," she said, out of breath.

"You can't mean that," Jill said shaking her head.

"Oh, I mean it alright. And if you can believe this, they're announcing it here, tonight!" she continued. "Their engagement!"

"That's impossible. No, it's insane! Why would they do such a thing?" Jill asked, her mouth open in astonishment.

"Because she's French, that's why. If they get engaged, and marry, she'll be able to come back to this country and stay," Alexis stated.

"Is that what he told you?" Jill asked.

"Well, basically. He said it had to be done to keep her here."

"What a rotten, mean, no good . . ., "Jill continued.

"Exactly. And to think that I went with my heart. That's the last time that I listen to Michael or anyone else for that matter. I should have known I'd get my heart stomped on again," Alexis said, tears now streaming down her face. "I had the proof right in front of me, but I didn't want to believe it."

"Now, Alexis, don't talk like that," Jill responded. "What do you want to do now? We have the ribbon cutting tomorrow."

"I'm leaving here, obviously, and tomorrow I'll just have to do my best to get through it." Alexis looked at Jill with deep sorrow. "I don't think I've ever been hurt like this ever. I didn't know that a human could be capable of something so horrible!"

"Let's get you out of here," Jill said as they started to walk out of the barn, avoiding conversations with the volunteers.

"Ladies and gentlemen," a voice boomed over the microphone. "I have a special announcement!" Colton stood on the stage, looking pale. "There is a very special person in my life that I want to acknowledge, that I love dearly, and tonight I want to share one of the most important announcements anyone can make. This is as much a surprise to me as anyone, but love has no agenda and no boundaries."

The crowd gathered around, anxious for the news. Chantelle stood on the side of the stage, beaming with excitement.

"My cousin Jackson here, has proposed to the lovely Chantelle. Jackson! Chantelle! Come up on this stage so that we can raise a glass to you both." Colton looked ill as he pushed himself to say the words.

Jill and Alexis were halfway to the car and stopped dead in their tracks. "Did he just say?" Alexis looked at Jill.

"He did!" Jill's eyes widened. "He just announced the engagement of Jackson and Chantelle!"

"Oh, my gosh!" Alexis looked at Jill and covered her mouth with her hand. "Oh, my gosh!" She started to laugh loudly. "She's marrying Jackson?" She laughed so hard she could hardly contain herself.

"Jackson? My Jackson?" Jill's face dropped. "I guess that explains his lack of interest in me."

"Jill! Do you get this? This whole time, Colton thought I'd be upset because Chantelle is going to be a part of the family!" She continued to laugh. "And that note! It was to Jackson!"

"What are you going to do?" Jill asked, watching Alexis laugh hysterically.

"I'm going back in there and I'm going to ask him to forgive me, that's what," Alexis said.

Alexis grabbed Jill's arm and rushed her inside of the barn. She then ran to the front of the room where Colton stood, looking deflated as Jackson and Chantelle stood on stage, kissing. The crowd was buzzing with excitement, clapping and toasting.

"Colton!" Alexis ran up to him, out of breath. He looked down at her surprised. "Colton, I have to apologize!"

He jumped off the stage and shook his head in confusion. "For what?"

"For doubting you. For doubting myself. I'll never do that again." She threw her arms around his neck and kissed him.

"I don't understand," he said bewildered.

"You don't have to!" she laughed. "I just made a darned fool out of myself!"

"So, you're not upset that Chantelle and Jackson are engaged? She's not going anywhere you know," he said still looking concerned.

"I know!" she laughed.

"And you aren't upset that she's going to be working at the vineyards?" he asked.

"No! I think it's great!" she hugged him.

"I'm totally confused." He looked at her as he stood with his arms around her waist.

"Can you forgive me?" she asked again.

"Yeah, I guess. Sure. Of course! Does this mean that we're Okay?"

"We're more than Okay," she smiled.

Colton grabbed her and swung her around before giving her a long kiss. "That's all I need to know!" He took a deep breath. "I thought I lost you! I didn't know how to tell you. It was all just so awkward. I mean Jackson and Chantelle?"

Alexis placed her hand on his mouth. "I know. Don't say another word." She kissed him again.

Jill stood at the edge of the dance floor watching them and shaking her head. She looked at Chantelle and Jackson on stage kissing then looked around the barn. There, across the room stood an attractive man in a cowboy hat and boots. He caught her eye, and tipped his hat. She tipped her hat back and winked.

"Well, hello cowboy!" Jill smiled to herself and gave him a girlish wave.

Chapter Fifteen

Alexis and Colton entered her Grandmother's room. "Grandma! You look beautiful!" Alexis exclaimed at the sight of her Grandmother, sitting in her dress and looking radiant.

"And aren't you a sight! Lovely! Just lovely!" She took Alexis's hand and squeezed it. "This is such a special day and I can't wait!"

"Neither can we," Alexis kissed her Gran and smiled. "Gran, you remember Colton?"

"Oh yes, my Harry's Grandson. It's so good to see you again, young man. Thank you for all that you've done for us. You and Alexis worked hard!"

"It was our pleasure," Colton smiled as he took her hand and squeezed it.

"Shall we?" Alexis asked as she took charge of her Grandmother's wheelchair.

The three stepped into the hallway where they could hear the voices and commotion of the gathering crowd. Along the way, Colton stopped at his Grandfather's room and wheeled him into the hall.

"My beautiful Fifi!" he smiled and reached out to take her hand. "Let's get this show on the road!"

Colton pushed his Grandfather while Alexis followed with her Grandmother. Down the hall, Mabel and her daughter, Annabel were approaching. Alexis waved. "Hello you two!"

"Annabel and I didn't want to miss this," Mabel said as they approached.

Alexis leaned down. "Annabel, you look very pretty today!" Annabel shyly smiled, folded her arms and rocked back and forth humming. "Let's get to the ceremony!"

They continued until they reached the patio doors that overlooked the new, magnificent garden. When the doors opened and the four appeared, the crowd began to clap. On the side of the door stood Jill who stepped forward.

"See? You did good," Jill whispered in Alexis's ear.

A gentleman stepped in front of the crowd with a microphone. "Ladies and gentlemen, as most of you know, I am James Dodd, the Creekside Manager. I know that you all are anxious to get to the celebration, so I won't keep you here long! We'd like to thank Alexis Bradford and Colton Winters for their dedication of time and love to this garden and the workshop that will now bring great joy to our Creekside residents. We want to thank all the wonderful Tranquility River volunteers that made this possible. Thank you, my friends, from the bottom of my heart. Now on to our exciting ribbon cutting." He handed Alexis a pair of scissors. "Miss Bradford, will you please do the honors?"

Alexis took the scissors and Colton placed his hand over hers. The two placed the ribbon between the blades, slicing it and prompting a loud cheer from the crowd.

"To Harry and Fifi," Colton smiled and kissed Alexis.

"To Harry and Fifi," Alexis laughed.

The couple turned to see their Grandparents clapping and smiling. Gus took Mary's hand in his and kissed it.

"All is right with the world," Alexis said.

"It certainly is," Colton agreed.

Alexis gave her Grandmother a kiss on the cheek. "Shall we take you inside for the reception?" she asked.

"Fifi? Let's go celebrate!" Gus boomed.

"Yes, Alexis. That would be lovely," her Grandmother responded.

Colton and Alexis wheeled the couple inside to a reception room full of food and refreshments.

"Annabel and I will make sure that they are taken care of," Mabel said. "Can we prepare a plate of food for you two?" she said to the elderly couple. They nodded their heads as Mabel and her young daughter grabbed plates and walked them to the table.

"Let's steal away for a moment," Colton said, as he took Alexis's hand and led her out to the garden. They stood for a moment, looking over the newly constructed pathways and garden beds.

"I have something I want to show you," Colton said. "Follow me." Colton walked her down a path to a quiet area where they sat on a concrete bench. He pulled a satchel off his shoulder and opened it. Inside were two glasses and a bottle of "Wooden Mistletoe" that he poured into each glass, handing her one.

"So, you thought that I was in love with Chantelle? That I was going to marry her?" He smiled.

"I feel like such a fool!" Alexis exclaimed.

"That'll teach you to read someone's mail," he grinned. "Jackson and Chantelle in love was shocking enough!"

"Can you forgive me?" she asked, with a look of innocence.

"I supposed." He paused and smiled. "If you'll do one thing."

"What's that?" Alexis asked, taking a sip of wine.

Colton reached into the satchel and pulled something out. He held it over her head. There swinging in his hand was the wooden mistletoe. "Marry me?"

She smiled as they placed their wine glasses down and kissed. "Yes."

Alexis smiled as she reminisced. She looked down at her hands, now wrinkled and frail. "And here we are, in the very same garden that you proposed," she said.

"Under the wooden mistletoe," Colton responded. "Yes, here we are, back where we started."

She smiled. "It certainly was an unusual beginning! Who would have guessed that Jackson and Chantelle would have been a perfect match? They had many happy years together!"

"She turned out to be a nice addition to the family," Colton reminded her.

"And a dear friend to me." She paused for a minute. "Yes, life is full of surprises."

"Alexis," Colton began, "my life with you was all that I dreamed it could be. We always knew, we were meant to be together." Colton stood and placed his wine glass on a bench. "Come, Alexis. Take my hand," he said as he extended his arm, waiting for her response. "Come with me."

She stared at him confused. "Get up?"

"Yes, get up, Alexis." He smiled and reached forward with his hand open. "It's Okay. It's time now."

Alexis looked at the stone patio beside her chair and watched as a deep red liquid spread and seeped into the cracks. Chards of glass were scattered and she realized that it was her wine glass, that now lay in pieces. "Oh! I dropped my wine. I didn't realize. . ."

"Take my hand, Alexis and get out of that chair," he insisted, paying no attention to the broken wine glass.

Alexis looked up at him, confused. "You know I can't stand up."

"But, you can, my dear," he said gently with an even bigger smile. "I'll help you."

Alexis looked back down at the broken glass and spreading pool of wine. She turned to Colton and reluctantly took his hand, slowly moving to the edge of her seat. She placed her feet on the ground and attempted to stand when she suddenly, found herself firmly planted, effortless and pain free.

"See?" He smiled.

"But," she stammered.

"Now look," he said as he gestured to the garden in front of her. "See it as I do."

The barren and cold garden was now teeming with flowers, fruits and vegetables, vibrant colors and fragrances. A warm breeze blew over her, knocking her shawl off her shoulders and to the ground. The flowers bent and danced.

"Oh! It's beautiful!" she gasped, amazed at the clarity of it all and the pure euphoria she now felt. The world now appeared brighter than she had ever experienced yet the intensity of the light did not bother her eyes. Sounds were sweet and melodic, as though the birds and insects of the world were singing a beautiful symphony. "Look!" she said, as she gazed down at her feet. "My shoes! They're gone!" She laughed loudly.

"Go ahead! Stick your toes in the grass and feel how soft it is," he said.

"I haven't felt the grass between my toes in so long," she said as a tear ran down her cheek.

"Come, my love," he said pulling on her hand. "There's more!

"Mama?" A young woman appeared through the doorway and rushed onto the patio. "Mama? Are you Okay?" The young woman bent down and quickly placed her hand on the shoulder of the body of the old woman that was now slumped backward in the wheel chair. The arm was extended out and limp. Below it, smashed on the stone patio was glass surrounded by a puddle of red wine that continued to trickle into the cracks of the cold stone.

Annabel quickly appeared. "Miss Angela? What happened?" she asked as she rushed over to the slumped body, the wooden mistletoe in her hand.

"I don't know! I found her like this," the young woman exclaimed.

Annabel grabbed the old woman's wrist, then pressed two fingers on her neck, feeling for a pulse. There was none. Anabelle looked at the young woman with a sorrowful expression. "She's gone," she whispered.

Angela fell to her knees next to the elderly woman. "Oh Mama," she whispered as she began to sob. "You're home." Tears streamed down her face. "You're with Daddy now." She took the woman's hand in hers and examined her face, her head rested on the back of the wheelchair as though she had nodded off to sleep. She had a peaceful expression and what appeared to be a slight smile. "I love you Mama. I love you." Angela placed her head on her mother's arm and wept.

"She's in her garden now," Annabel said, as her eyes welled up with tears. "She's out there," she said pointing to the garden.

Alexis and Colton now in the midst of the thick field of flowers and herbs turned to look back. Alexis stopped and hesitated. "They'll be fine," Colton said as he placed his arm around her shoulder. "Angela is capable and we'll watch over her like I watched over you," he said.

"We will?" Alexis asked.

"Of course. She'll never be far away," he smiled. "Now come, young lady. Care to join me for a glass of wine? At the vineyards at our favorite spot?" he asked. Alexis smiled and kissed him. "I've been waiting for that for some time now!" he smiled and squeezed her hand.

"Oh, wait!" Alexis stopped and looked back. "My mistletoe!"

"Dear, we have no use for that here. It's Angela's now. She'll take care of it and its legacy along with the vineyards. Everything is in good hands. We taught her well."

Alexis saw Annabel staring out into the garden, holding the wooden mistletoe. "Can Annabel see us?" Alexis asked. Her face no longer showed wrinkles and her skin glowed like it did many years before.

"I think so," Colton answered as he waved at Annabel in the distance who stood staring. Annabel waved back and smiled, tears streaming.

"Good bye Annabel," Alexis quietly said. "Good bye my dear Angela. We shall love and watch over you always."

The couple turned and walked deep into the garden, holding hands and disappeared into the mist of the woods.

Annabel waved, "Goodbye my dear friends."

CPSIA information can be obtained
at www.ICGtesting.com
Printed in the USA
LVHW110033200919
631651LV00014B/21/P

9 781478 751892